Shameless

PLAYBOYS IN LOVE SERIES

Gina L. Maxwell

Entangled Publishing, LLC
2614 South Timberline Road
Suite 109
Fort Collins, CO 80525
Visit our website at www.entangledpublishing.com.

Scorched is an imprint of Entangled Publishing, LLC.

Edited by Liz Pelletier
Cover design by Heather Howland
Cover art from Shutterstock

Manufactured in the United States of America

First Edition May 2016

entangled
scorched

To my amazing readers,
Every word I write is for you.
Love, G

Chapter One

JANE

If such a thing as a Landlords of Chicago Convention existed, and said convention had an award for Worst Landlord of a Multi-Unit Building, mine would win by a landslide. A freaking landlord landslide.

Cursing his name for the umpteenth time in the last half hour, I wrap a Band-Aid around the cut in my thumb I'd acquired trying to unclog the pipes under my bathroom sink. God forbid Walter would actually do his job and call a plumber for me.

Since I'd moved into my small apartment in the South Shore area, my hot water heater, oven, and window A/C unit had all taken a crap at one point or another—just a few of the perks of living in a building so old that it predates the invention of the elevator—and each time it had taken Walter weeks to get them fixed.

But I'm nothing if not independent and self-reliant—traits born of being the child of workaholic parents. I'd managed to repair my garbage disposal and replace the tank assembly in my toilet by browsing the almighty Google and ignoring all my girly squeamishness at the ick factor of both. Neither instance had been pretty, but it wasn't anything a hot shower and the satisfaction of a job well done couldn't wash away.

Unfortunately, my stupid bathroom sink pipes aren't going to be added to that list of accomplishments anytime soon. I don't know if the slip nuts (thank you, Google Images) had been screwed on by the Incredible Hulk or fused in place by the lesser-known supervillain Rust Man. Either way, those suckers aren't budging for a mortal female with minimal experience handling a pipe wrench. (Feel free to insert dirty joke here.)

I glare at the standing water in the sink, hands on my hips, willing it to magically go down. I'm so focused on trying to Jedi-mind-trick the bastard into submission that I jump when my phone rings. Jogging into the living room, I snatch up the cell and answer as I plop onto the couch.

"Hey, you," I say, greeting my best friend Addison Paige. "Aren't you supposed to be burning the midnight oil?"

"It's only seven p.m., but I'm sure I'll still be here when midnight rolls around," Addison says wryly. "You writing your paper?"

I laugh. Calling my masters thesis on social work a *paper* was like calling the Taj Mahal a chapel. I've been working on it for two years, and I'm almost—*almost*—done. Turning it in is the last step in getting my dual degree. Then I can finally get a job in my field and start making some real money instead of the piddly-ass wages I make as an intern and part-time waitress. (And then move.)

"Surprisingly, no," I say. "I'm still trying to fix the clog in my bathroom sink, but all I've managed to do is pinch my thumb. Luckily, I managed to staunch the flow before I bled out all over the floor."

"Damn good thing, because if you die before I get my *fun* friend back, I'll kill you myself."

"You know what I love about you?" I ask, laying the sarcasm on thick. "It's that you make complete sense when you threaten me. I think it's what makes you the best lawyer ever."

"And I love that you love that about me. And also that you repeatedly tell me I'm the best lawyer ever instead of acknowledging my pathetic peon status. This boys club of a law firm isn't going to give me my own cases anytime soon."

"Nonsense. It's only a matter of time before they see your brilliance and make you a partner," I say with confidence. "Wait—since when am I not your 'fun' friend? I'm fun."

"Seriously? When was the last time you went out? For *fun*. Not for school or work or any other life-sucking activity. Like, to a dance club or a bar or a fucking baseball game? I don't know…*anything*."

I open my mouth to respond with a list of all the things I've done recently that qualified—because surely there *is* a list—but come up with nothing. I honestly can't remember the last time I went out to be social. I've hung out with Addison, but that was more lunch dates and Netflix than clubbing and cavorting.

"Um…"

"Exactly," Addison crows.

Okay, so she's not wrong. It's been a while since I've had a social life and an even *longer* while since I've had a sex life, which makes me grateful she didn't bring that particular nugget up. My recent hermit status may have slipped my notice, but I'm painfully aware of how long it's been (for-freaking-*ever*) since I've been satisfied by someone other than myself.

Completing my masters coursework in two years instead of three, and then replacing school hours with work hours, doesn't leave me with any time to invest in a relationship. I'm all for casual flings or even one-night stands, but the handful of forays hadn't been worth shaving, much less the Brazilians I'd splurged on. After my last underwhelming sexual rendezvous, I decided that I wouldn't drop trou for anyone else unless I'm positive it'll be worth the pain of getting my pubic hair ripped out by the roots by a sadistic woman armed with strips of hot wax. If you've ever subjected yourself to that particular brand of cosmetic torture, you know that's setting the bar for sexual excellence pretty high.

So while I wait for Mr. Mind-Blowing-In-The-Sack, I bought a Hitachi Magic Wand—God bless the misguided man who thought he designed a great neck massager—and became a frequent purveyor of internet porn.

That's right. I'm a closet porn addict.

Don't judge me. It gets the job done. With the right video, I can be turned on in minutes. Then, depending on my mood, I'll either watch several to build the anticipation, or simply dive right in and get myself off in what I call an "express O." Bing, bam, boom, done.

But like I said, it's not something I'm ready to share with the class. Not even with Addison. Not because I think she'll judge me—that girl is all for owning your freak flag and letting it fly—but because I'd inevitably have to answer questions about how often do I watch it (several times a week), and what kind do I like (the rougher, the better), and do I have a favorite porn star (hands down, Harley Hummer). I'd just rather not get into the gory details of how I take the edge off my sexual frustrations, thank you very much.

"What's it called when the lawyer is being an obnoxious asshat?" I ask my best friend. "Is it contempt? I find you in contempt of court, *and* I object. Your argument is erroneous. I don't need a good time right now, I just need someone to fix my pipes."

"Yeah, your *lady* pipes," she jokes. "Things are probably just as rusted shut down there as they are under your sink."

Actually, since I don't use a dildo of any kind, it's highly likely. "Okay, that's it," I say, laughing in spite of myself, "I'm hanging up. You need to get back to work, and I need to do anything other than talk to you at the moment."

Sighing dramatically, Addison acquiesces. "Fine, killjoy. Does this mean you don't want the number of a handyman who came highly recommended to me?"

I sit up a little straighter, perking up at the words "highly recommended." Growing up in the digital age as I have, you'd think that I would trust online reviews of products and services. But things on the internet can be bought or faked. I'd much rather take the word of someone I know, and I'm ready to cry "uncle" and be done with this whole situation. "Who recommended him?"

"Rebecca, one of our paralegals. She said he's worth every cent and more. I believe her exact words were 'the best ever.'"

That sounds promising, so I grab the pen and pad of paper from the side table. "Okay, what's the number? I'll give him a call tomorrow."

"One sec, I've got another call coming in. Hang on." And with a *click* the line went silent.

I lean back on the couch, staring at the spidery ceiling paint, following the bigger cracks and admiring how they fan out with reckless abandon. Of course, they probably knew what I knew: no way was I standing on a ladder and painting upside down to fix them. When Addison clicks back over, I tell her, "All right. I'm ready for the number of my miracle plumber."

"No need," she replies. "I just called and paid in advance. Consider it an early birthday present. He'll be there in about an hour."

"What? It's too late for anyone to be making house calls

on a Friday night."

"Riiiiight. Because everyone's shit only breaks between the hours of eight and five on weekdays." Addison is just as fond of sarcasm as I am. It's one of the reasons we make such great friends.

"Point taken, but you still shouldn't have called." I hate it when she tries to pay for things. Peon or not, she makes a good living as a lawyer and likes to make up dumb reasons why I should let her pick up the tab on stuff. "My birthday's not even for another six months."

"So then it's a *half* birthday present. Hasn't anyone ever told you not to look a gift-friend in the mouth? Have some wine, read a book, tweeze your eyebrows. I don't care, as long as you let the man do what he's hired for when he gets there, okay?"

"Yes, Mother," I say with the tone of an audible eye roll. But then I add a sincere, "Thanks, Addie."

"You're welcome, babe. Oh, and make sure you call me tomorrow and tell me all the juicy details. Ciao!"

Before I can comment on the ridiculousness of anything involving a middle-aged man with plumber's crack being "juicy," she hangs up. Belatedly, I realize I never even got the name of the guy or his business. I almost call her back to ask, but figure it's not a big deal. The odds of someone showing up coincidentally under false pretenses as a handyman in disguise are pretty much nil.

It's been a long week, and that glass of wine Addison mentioned is suddenly calling my name.

Blowing out a deep breath, I stand and head to the kitchen where I have an open bottle of red. For once, I'm going to take my friend's advice: enjoy a glass of wine and a book while I wait for the "best ever handyman" to arrive and do his thing. Now that I know help is on the way, I'm really looking forward to getting my pipes fixed.

Chapter Two

CHANCE

I'm so not in the fucking mood to dance tonight, much less do a one-on-one sesh with some horny, middle-aged woman who'll probably angle for sex afterward. Normally, I'd be all over that shit. Hooking up with clients is one of the bennies of being a stripper-for-hire. I dance and make their panties wet, then they do the same to my dick. It's a win-win.

People might think less of me for having that attitude, but the way I see it, it's no different than hooking up with someone in a club. Did I say "in" a club? I meant *from* a club. But I've done it *in* a club, too. I'm not too particular on the when and where, and I'm sure as hell not shy.

Don't make the mistake of thinking I'm some kind of gigolo, though. The money I get as a private stripper is strictly for my stripping services, not for any extracurricular activities that might happen afterward. That's something different entirely. The guys who work for me at Playboys 4 Hire refer to them as "bonus dances." Bonus for the women, and definitely a bonus for us.

But tonight, I'm just not feeling it. For probably the first time since I started P4H with my best friends Roman Reeves and Austin Massey during our days as college students up at UW Madison, I'd rather be nursing a beer or six while playing Call of Duty than get groped as someone shoves money into my Tommy Hilfigers.

My head's not in the game. It's wrapped up in some issues I have with my other company—the construction company I've grown over the last several years using the knowledge I gained with my expensive-as-hell business degree. I have a huge contract currently stalled by the city, bound up with more fucking red tape than I could cut through with a Sawzall. Now we're way behind on schedule, and it's got me on edge. Not a great mood to be in when you have to seduce a woman, whether it's real or fantasy.

I pause in front of the apartment number I was given and do a quick mental dump. I need to get in the right head space if I'm going to pull off the job without the client realizing I have shit on my mind other than dry humping her into next week.

Showtime. Rolling my shoulders back in my navy blue handyman coveralls, I raise my fist, knock on the door, and wait for my client to let me in.

"Yes?" a feminine voice calls through the door.

I notice the absence of a peephole and frown. The place is old, but there's no excuse for not updating the apartments with some basic safety features. Still, she *is* expecting me, and clients enjoy the fantasy right from the start.

"Ms. Wendall, I'm the handyman," I say. "I'm here to give you a hand with whatever you need."

I expect the door to whip open. Instead, there's a long pause. "That's awfully vague." Her tone sounds suspicious. "What were you called for specifically?"

Smart girl, making me prove I'm her expected guest without making me break character. When she called earlier, she'd said she "needed a handyman to fix her pipes." Sometimes clients prefer to give us storylines to follow. None of us mind—after all, it's our job to sell them the fantasy, whatever that may be.

"To fix your pipes," I answer. "But I won't do you any good with this door"—I hear the lock roll through its tumbler a second before the door swings open—"between us," I finish absently as I try to process what I'm seeing.

What I'd expected—or rather *who* I'd expected—was a woman wearing lust like a heavy fur coat that practically swallows her whole. A woman with very little clothing, who would eye-fuck the shit out of me before moving aside to finally let me in so we can get on with my reason for being here.

What I *got* is a woman wearing yoga pants, fuzzy slipper socks, and a zipped up Loyola University hoodie. Long brown hair is tied up in some messy knot thing on her head. To complete her at-home-don't-care look, she's wearing rectangular dark-rimmed glasses and no makeup. Or at least, none that I can tell from the brief look I get at her face. She hasn't even glanced up from the thick hardcover book in her hands before she turns away and walks farther into the apartment, leaving me standing in the hallway like an idiot with my dick in my hands.

Shaking off the initial surprise, I step inside, closing and locking the door behind me. As she passes it, she points down a hallway that branches off of the tiny dining area next to the kitchen. "The bathroom is that way. Just let me know if you need me for anything."

Suddenly, it clicks. Jane Wendall (that's the name she'd given on the phone, even though the one on the credit card was Addison Paige) wants to be seduced. She wants to be that unsuspecting, naive girl seduced by the handyman who has other things on his mind than the "problem" she'd called him about. Damn, I'd almost blown it by asking her what she wanted me to do.

"Sure thing," I say as I cross to the dining table, keeping a discreet eye on her. She's doing an excellent job of ignoring me. If I didn't know any better, I'd think she really wasn't interested in what I'm doing.

I set down my old red toolbox and open it up. It doesn't hold the kind of tools one would typically find, but rather the tools of *this* trade. A few bottles of water (for drinking and/or pouring over my body), a fresh can of whipped cream I picked up on the way, a change of clothes, a portable speaker that's synced with the playlists on my phone, and for the occasional "bonus dances," some flavored lube and a box of condoms.

Intuition says I probably only need the speaker and a bottle of water to drink afterward for this one. Though, if I'm being honest, something about Jane/Addison is seriously doing it for me. I hope she's just feigning disinterest, and maybe, if things click between us like I think they might, we can explore things on a more real level after I dance for her.

Tonight actually has the potential to not suck.

"Mind if I listen to some music?"

She glances up from her book, her glasses now dangling from the earpiece held between her teeth, and furrows her brow like she's forgotten why I'm there. My cock must be on the fritz because her blatant disregard for my presence makes it twitch with interest.

"I know you're reading, but music really helps me when I…" Pause for dramatic effect. "Work."

Jane sets her glasses on her open book. A slow smile spreads over her face and gut-checks me like a hockey player. It's absolutely radiant, with straight white teeth and full pink lips that stretch into a perfect crescent. I'd thought she was attractive in that captivating school nerd kind of way, but damn… Her smile launches her to a level of sexiness I can't even name.

"Sure," she says. "I don't mind. I can easily tune things out when I need to."

Yeah, I've seen evidence of that already, and I don't like it. Don't like her tuning me out. I want her tuned *in*. To every move and every touch.

Eager to get started, I set the small speaker on the table, sync my favorite playlist, and look over to where she's sitting tucked into the corner of her couch, already seemingly engrossed again in that damn book. If she keeps this act going much longer, my ego will be in serious danger of deflating.

I saunter over, my steps instinctively matching the sultry beats of "Earned It" by The Weeknd as I let the music roll through me. I've always loved dancing; always been good at it. Dancing for horny women and making bank for a few hours of fun is a no-brainer.

Planting my feet in front of her, I wait for her to look up, which she does. She starts eye-level at my thighs then gradually moves north. The farther her gaze climbs, the wider her eyes get, until she reaches my face. Gingerly, Jane—I've decided that's what I'm calling her; I like it better, and something about it suits her—slides her glasses back on, and her mouth falls slack.

Fucking finally. I try to hide my smile at her reaction, but it probably comes off as a cocky smirk. That works, too, considering I'm playing the part of the cocky (pun intended) handyman about to ravish my unsuspecting client.

"Do you need something?" she asks, her voice cracking at the end.

"Yeah, I do. I need you to check out my pipe wrench. Make sure it's in working order to your satisfaction."

"Excuse me?"

"You heard me, beautiful." I toss her book to the side, pull her ass to the edge of the couch cushion, and then step between her legs. "I want your eyes on my big, hard tool."

Before she's able to get out a word of protest—and she *is* about to protest, choosing to play her role to the bitter end—I move my hips to the beat of the music and yank the front of my coveralls open, the sound of the metallic snaps popping like distant fireworks. I shrug the top half from my shoulders to hang around my legs, revealing a skin-tight wife-beater that isn't long for this world.

Grabbing both of her hands, I press them to my chest and almost groan at the warmth radiating from her soft skin. I flex my pecs beneath her palms and then slide them slowly down and over the ridges of my abs. I hear her quiet gasp, and it makes all the hard work of maintaining this kind of muscle definition damn worth it.

When our joined hands reach my hips, I start to twist them from side to side with fluid movements; letting her feel the beat of the music as it rolls through me, and she listens to my body make her the kind of promises whispered in the dark between sweat-dampened sheets.

Jane is clearly flustered, and it doesn't even seem faked. Maybe she's more innocent than I'd assumed. In fact, studying her reactions, I know exactly the kind of girl she is. In a party of women where strippers are the entertainment, she's the quiet one in the back hoping like hell none of the dancers notice her, and blushing like crazy—like she is now—as she allows herself to fantasize about what it would be like to get fucked by a man like that.

What those girls don't know is their shy and embarrassed nature is exactly what makes the dancers single them out. Nine times out of ten, a guy would rather dance for the shy girls than the ones trying to dry hump their junk.

"Whoa whoa whoa," she says, freeing her hands and

scuttling off the end of the couch. "I think there's been a mistake. I'm sorry if I blinked weirdly earlier and you thought I was winking or whatever, but I wasn't coming on to you, I promise. I just want my sink fixed."

I advance with a couple of quick steps, crowding her back against the wall and forcing her to crane her head back to keep eye contact. "Just your sink, huh? So that means you don't want any of this?" To demonstrate what "this" is, I undulate over her much smaller frame. I have to widen my stance to make our heights work better, then I press my chest into hers and roll down from there. Sternum to stomach to pelvis, and holy Christ, I can feel the heat from her pussy radiating through her thin pants.

"Oh my God. Um... I can't believe I'm saying this." Squeezing her eyes shut briefly, she clears her throat. "No, thank you. Just unclogging the sink would be great."

Perplexed, I take a step back and stare hard at her, trying to find traces of excitement in her expression that belie the words coming from her mouth. Finally, I decide it's better to err on the side of caution than wind up with a sexual harassment suit for Roman to deal with. Time to break character.

"Ms. Paige, maybe you have a different idea of what a Handyman Special is. It'd help out a lot if I understood what exactly you want from me."

"Ms. Paige? No, I'm not..." She appears confused for all of two seconds before she hides her face with her hands and whispers, "Oh my God, I'm going to kill her. Absolutely *kill* her."

Chapter Three

JANE

"Come again?" he asks in a voice hot enough to melt butter.

It was a simple, perfectly appropriate phrase used to ask another person to repeat themselves. But what do I hear? I hear him ask if he should give me another orgasm, as though he's already given me the first one, and is now curious if I might want more. Like a waiter inquiring whether he should refill my wineglass. *Yes, please.*

Jesus, Janey, get a grip already. Clearing my throat as delicately as possible, I use my index finger to push on the bridge of my glasses before forcing myself to meet his eyes. Those denim-blue, you'll-do-anything-I-say eyes… *Damn it.*

"I'm sorry, but I think there's been a mistake." *And by that, I mean my friend has a death wish because she sent over a stripper instead of a plumber.*

A single brow arches as the opposite corner of his mouth ticks up. It should make him look off-balance or crooked. It doesn't. It makes him panty-meltingly gorgeous. "Are you trying to tell me you didn't order a Handyman Special?"

"Technically, I didn't order anything. My friend did. And unless a 'Handyman Special'"—I use air quotes around the obvious euphemism—"means you're here to fix my bathroom sink while fully clothed, then that's exactly what I'm telling you."

I sound deflated even to my own ears, but that would mean that I actually *want* him to give me whatever is included in his version of a Handyman Special. And that's fricking ridiculous because I'm not into strippers. Not that I have a ton of experience with them, but a group of us went to a male strip club for kicks and giggles a few years ago, and I had way more giggles than kicks.

But *this* stripper… This sexy Norse god could double for Chris Hemsworth in *Thor,* with his dirty blond hair brushing the tops of his rounded shoulders, and his half-lidded bedroom eyes that won't stop undressing me wherever they land.

His skin has the natural bronze hue that surfers are blessed with from spending their days in the sun. It doesn't have the glistening shine from oil, but it doesn't appear dry either, like maybe he has a moisturizing regimen that keeps it supple and oh-so-touchable, which is in direct contrast to the calluses I felt on his fingers and palms when he touched me.

I want desperately to reach out and test my theory. To run my hands over the swells and valleys of his muscles, this time without the teasing barrier of his shirt, but I manage to keep my hands to myself. Just barely. Instead, I let my eyes do the touching, taking in all the sexy details, like the tiny points of his nipples straining against the thin material of his tank, and the trim chest hair peeking above the low scoop neck.

Damn, that's hot. I have a thing for the rustic, manly type. I'll take blue collar over white any day of the week, and Mr. Handyman here is as blue as they come.

"Let me see if I have this right," he says, folding his

arms across his wide chest and interrupting my mental drool session. "You're Jane Wendall, and your friend—Addison Paige—called me to come over here and show you a good time, but she told *you* that she was sending over an actual handyman to fix your sink?"

I sigh in frustration, though whether from the situation or my sexual dry spell, I'm not sure. Probably both. "That about sums it up."

"Wanna know what I think, Ms. Wendall?"

"Jane," I correct. "And no, probably not."

"I think you *do* want me to show you a good time."

I scoff. "Then you would be wrong, Mister…"

"Chance."

"Mr. Chance."

"Just Chance."

"Fine, Just Chance," I say, "but you're still wrong."

"Am I, though?"

Leaning in, he braces one hand high above my head and hooks the thumb of his other into the front of his coveralls, tugging them down just enough that I catch a glimpse of a goody trail that disappears behind the elastic of his underwear. And now all I can think about is yanking them off to see what kind of equipment he's working with.

I wonder what it would feel like to have a man like him driving between my legs, filling me with his big cock. My breasts grow heavy beneath my hoodie and the rougher underside of the cotton abrades my sensitive nipples as they tighten into small buds.

Oh my God. I need to cut down on the porn.

"See something you like, Jane?"

Caught ogling his crotch while letting my body run rampant with the sordid thoughts in my mind, I snap my head up so fast I almost smack it against the wall. "Nope, not a thing," I say, my voice pitched high with guilt. "Not that you're not, um… What I mean is, if I were in the market for that kind of…something…then I'm sure I'd like yours. But I'm not. In the market. For, you know…that. So…"

Holy shit, shut up shut up shut up.

"You're really sexy when you're flustered, you know that?"

Oh, awesome. A reality check.

There are several words I might use to describe my current appearance—haggard, bedraggled, or even sloppy to name a few—but *sexy* is definitely not one of them. On the rare occasions I let Addison play makeover with my face, shove me into a mini-dress, and force me to wear my uncomfortable contacts, I *might* pass for sexy, but mostly I just look like the girl-next-door who's trying too hard.

And to think I was starting to get all hot and bothered by Mr. Just Chance. Le sigh. "Look, you can drop the act, okay? I'm sorry you came all the way out for nothing, but now we both know I was Punk'd by my friend, so you can pack up your stuff and head on to your next customer."

"I don't have anywhere else to be," he says, smiling like the fox that's cornered the hen. "And what makes you think I'm putting on an act? Because I promise you, I'm not. Not anymore."

I let out a sarcastic chuckle. "Right, okay. You must have a thing for nerdy girls who look like they haven't showered, then."

He arches that damn arrogant brow again and gives me a quick once-over, making my skin tingle as though he'd physically trailed his fingers down my naked body. "Funny…" His mention of humor contradicts the serious expression on his handsome face. "You don't smell like you haven't showered."

"What? No." I'm starting to get pissy. Sexual frustration plus self-denial of sexy stranger equals an unhappy Janey.

If he doesn't leave soon, I'm going to make a total ass of myself when I give in to his act and become one of probably hundreds who have built his ego to mammoth proportions. I'm only human. "I said I *look* like I haven't. If you must know, I showered a few hours ago. Thankfully, there's nothing wrong with *those* pipes."

"Let's see." Before I can say anything, he dips his head and sniffs me, causing a pack of pterodactyls to kick up in my stomach. The world goes dark as my eyes drift shut, and I inhale sharply when his nose grazes the side of my neck, making my skin come alive in its wake. "Yep. Definitely showered. You smell fresh and edible as fuck."

"I do?" My words are little more than a breathy sigh, my voice sounding foreign even to me. But that's okay because I finally figured out that I must have fallen asleep on the couch and this is all a dream. Things like this, where a handyman (or stripper dressed as a handyman—semantics) seduces his client instead of fixing her sink, don't happen in real life, and even if they do, they sure as shit never happen to regular girls like me.

"Yeah," he rumbles next to my ear, the vibrations sinking into the very marrow of my bones and making me weak. "You fucking do."

I feel myself leaning in more than I'm leaning away now. He's so warm and hard and huge, it's like he has his own gravitational pull, and resisting suddenly seems futile. The hand that has been anchored in his coveralls comes up to frame my face, and the way his calluses softly scrape my cheek makes me shiver. I let him turn my head until our mouths are lined up and his breath mingles with mine.

Dear God, I want to kiss him. I want to taste him, to discover if his silver tongue lends itself to more than just lip service. I don't think I've ever wanted something so badly in my entire life.

"Jane." I love the way he says my name, raspy and strained and kind of drawn out, like a plea. Or a question of permission…

I answer him in kind, whispering the final dissolution of my resolve with a single word. "Chance."

He starts to close the small gap, and I close my eyes in preparation for what will surely be the best kiss of my life… when my cell phone rings.

We yank apart like teens getting walked in on by their parents, and I'm quick to step around him so he can't see my cheeks flood with the embarrassment I feel at having damn near thrown myself at a stripper who's been paid to "show me a good time" by my *ex*-best friend.

"Speak of the devil," I mutter and send Addison to voicemail before turning my phone on silent and dropping it onto the couch. I need a full night's sleep before dealing with her. She probably thinks her little surprise is over with by now and decided she couldn't wait for tomorrow to hear all the "juicy details." Now her parting words to me earlier make perfect sense. Have I mentioned I'm going to kill her?

"I'll make you a deal," the deep voice behind me says.

Steeling myself against his charms (aka, his godlike body and off-the-charts sex appeal), I turn around. Jesus, did he somehow get *hotter* in the last few seconds? Chance is like my own personal kryptonite. If I have any hope of surviving this with my dignity intact, I need to keep plenty of distance between us and kindly dismiss him from my apartment.

No problem. Here I go.

"What kind of deal?"

Damn it!

"The kind where I fix your sink, and you let me dance for you."

That gets my attention. "Fix my sink?"

He nods. "If you let me dance for you afterward."

"How do you even know you can fix it?"

"Let's say I've been around the handyman block."

I snort. "I'll just bet you have."

Ignoring my tiny barb, he asks, "Do we have a deal?"

I narrow my eyes and cross my arms, preparing to haggle. I really, *really* want my sink fixed. "So, you'll do that, and all I have to do is let you dance for me? As in, from across the room?"

Chance crosses his arms like mine, though he actually appears intimidating whereas I'm lucky if I pass for indifferent. "As in, you sit, and I dance the way I always do. *Very* up-close and *very* personal."

Shit shit shit. There's no universe in which Chance grinds all over me where we don't end up screwing like rabbits. Not if what happened a few minutes ago is anything to go by. But as much as I'd love to let go and have myself a much needed fling, a small part of me can't help but wonder how many clients he hooks up with on a regular basis, and the idea of being another hash mark on his G-string doesn't sit well with me.

In the end, I decide to go with the lesser of two evils—resisting sex-on-a-very-big-stick versus living with backed up water so gross it could be a middle school science experiment.

"Okay, we have a deal," I say, holding out my hand for a businesslike shake. "My sink for your dance."

Chance steps forward and takes my hand, dwarfing it with his massive paw. But instead of shaking it like I intended, he lifts the front of his tank with his other hand and drags my palm down his bare chest, over his ripped abs, and continues past where his coveralls hang low on his hips. I snatch my hand away like his package is a hot pan, before it gets a mind of its own and starts groping instead of behaving.

My kryptonite chuckles. "Just thought you might want a sample of what's to come."

There he goes again, using the word "come" all innocently, like he isn't trying to put thoughts of orgasms in my head. Okay, he probably isn't doing that in the least. But as he winks at me and ambles toward the bathroom, I have to wonder if maybe that wasn't his intention after all. Oh, and I was right. His skin? Incredibly supple and touchable.

I. Am so. Screwed.

Chapter Four

CHANCE

Jane, Jane, Jane.

I love her name. From the moment she opened the door, I knew it suited her better than Addison. Funny, but I've always thought of "Jane" as a sort of vanilla name. It sounds boring and plain, just like you'd expect the person who answered to it to be. I mean, the term Plain Jane has to come from somewhere, right? Stereotypes are stereotypes for a reason.

But *this* Jane is the fucking exception to that rule. And yet, I can't put my finger on why. It's not like she's sexy in the vixen sort of way, with smoky makeup and clothing that fits like a second skin. She's kind of a disaster, actually, and a geeky one at that. But underneath the glasses, messy hair, and stained college hoodie, she exudes a kind of sexual energy that defies the message her outward appearance gives off, and it's killing me knowing it's just beneath the surface.

And that's the very reason I pushed for the dance. Her mouth—or more accurately, her brain—is saying she doesn't want me, doesn't want to explore the heat sparking between us. But those big brown eyes of hers are saying the exact opposite. They were glassy and nearly black, and I know that if I stuck my hand down the front of her yoga pants, I'd find her wet and good to go. Now I have an insatiable need to peel back that layer of inhibition and see what she's capable of when nothing's holding her back. The best shot I have at doing that is dancing for her. Stripping is an art of seduction, and I'm damn good at it, so I'm going to use that to my advantage.

I find the bathroom easily enough and take in the scene. She's tried fixing it herself but obviously had no luck, since the sink is half-full with murky water. The cabinet doors of the vanity are both open, with a plastic bucket placed beneath the P-trap, and a shiny, new pipe wrench is on the counter. Her laptop is either off or in sleep mode on the lid of the closed toilet, and I'd bet a month's income she has a "fixing clogged sinks" page pulled up on a how-to website.

I smile. I like that she's self-reliant...and that thought has me frowning. Because why the hell should I care if she's self-reliant or a spoiled princess? I shouldn't.

I don't. I'm not interested in her more than how she'll feel squeezing my dick as I fuck us both into oblivion. She's no different than any other woman I hook up with.

Satisfied with that little reassurance, I kneel down in front of the vanity. It comes as no surprise that she hadn't been successful. The building is old as hell, and the landlord apparently hasn't put any money into updating the plumbing. Instead of the much easier to work with PVC, Jane's sink still has the original steel pipes. The slip nuts are likely rusted to the point of nice-fucking-try, and it'll take a hell of a lot of torque to get them moving. Something a little thing like Jane wouldn't have, no matter how valiant her efforts, but hopefully I won't have that same problem.

Grabbing the wrench, I settle onto the floor and get into a

position to throw my weight behind it. I clamp it on to the pipe and start pushing. Shit, it's really on there good. The wrench moves a tiny bit, but it's not because the nut loosens. The tool is turning on the nut itself, losing traction, and stripping the outside of it. I release the pipe and try it from the left side. Pulling it toward me, I try keeping the balance between torque and finesse so I won't strip the nut.

Slowly…*so slowly*…it gives way, loosening a hair more every few seconds. I hold my breath and grit my teeth, and though I'm not a praying kind of guy, I may even toss up a literal Hail Mary in hopes it'll do some good.

Finally, the nut comes free, and it's as if the opposing team in a game of tug-of-war counted to three and let go all at once. I almost land flat on my back but manage to catch myself at the last second. I must've jostled her laptop because I hear it whir to life, and a second later the screen lights up on a webpage titled "Lose the Loser and Fix Your Own Sink: a How-To Guide for the Independent Woman."

Bull's-eye. I chuckle and shake my head. I'd been dead-on, and having it confirmed is an entertaining pat on the back. One thing that being a stripper has taught me is how to read women. Put me in a room of two dozen women, and just by watching them for five minutes, I can point out things about each of them that typically only their friends and acquaintances will know—their personalities, their likes and dislikes, and sometimes even their habits. It's a talent that's come in handy more times than I can count.

I grab the top of the laptop to shut it, but the screen switches from helpful guide to a frozen image of a naked man fisting a woman's hair as he gags her with his cock.

What. The. Fuck.

How the hell did that even happen? At first I think I might've clicked an ad that opened up the popular site, Porn Hub, but the only thing I touched was the very top with my thumb—

Oh, no way. Testing my theory that her laptop is the kind with a touchscreen, I poke at the center, and the video comes to life, thankfully with the sound muted.

Holy shit, I was right. Which means I'd accidentally opened up one of the tabs in Jane's browser.

And *that* means one *very* important thing: Jane watches porn.

And not just any kind of porn, I realize as I scroll through her browsing history. She watches the rough-as-fuck, choke-me-with-your-cock, call-me-your-slut kind of porn.

Someone alert the media that Hell has officially frozen over. Because I think I'm in love.

Chapter Five

JANE

I'm on my second glass of Cabernet when Chance walks—
no, *struts*—into the room, his eyes pinning me to my place
in the corner of the couch. As he passes the switch on the
wall that controls the overhead lights in both my living and
dining areas, he flicks them off. Now the only light is coming
from the small table lamp next to me, and I suddenly realize
I should've made rules or stipulations for this portion of our
deal. Like, all lights on, with at least two feet between us, and
for the duration of one song, not to exceed three and a half
minutes. Then maybe I'd actually have a decent chance at
resisting Chance.

"It's fixed?" I ask as he stops in front of me. "Just like
that?"

"Yep. Just like that. It was one hell of a clog, but
everything's running free and clear now. You can go check it
if you want."

I know I should, but I can't seem to make my limbs

move. Besides, I'd heard the water running, so it's pretty safe to assume he'd flushed the pipe after clearing whatever had been blocking it. But even if he didn't really fix it, what was I going to do? It's not like he was a *real* handyman I'd hired to do the job, and I'd be no worse off than I was before Addie came up with this harebrained scheme.

I suppose I'd be able to call off the dance portion of the deal if he hadn't held up his end by fixing my sink, but the wine has loosened me up enough that my inner horndog now rules, and no way in hell am I turning down the opportunity to have this man as my private dancer, if only for one song.

He's tied the sleeves of his coveralls into a knot at his lower abdomen, I guess so they won't fall off, because God forbid he puts them back on and covers up all that yummy goodness. I raise the glass to my lips and then drain the rest of the robust red wine as he comes to a stop in front of me. He holds my gaze, takes the glass from my hands, and sets it on the end table next to the stack of *Cosmo* magazines.

"Twenty ways to make him beg for it, huh?"

I blink up at him. "Excuse me?"

He picks up the top magazine and holds it out for me to see. Sure enough, the lead story of that issue touts untold secrets of how to bring a man to his knees. "So, tell me, Jane," he says with a cocky smirk. "How *do* you make a guy beg for it?"

"I wouldn't know," I answer, my pulse kicking up a notch. "I don't actually read them."

I snatch it from his grasp and place it back where it belongs, cover side down. Not so that he can't see the articles advertised, but because the sexy model in her mini-dress with her hair blowing in "the wind" and the *do me* expression on her flawless face makes me look like a hobo in comparison.

"Then what's with the mountain on the table?"

"I like looking at the fashion pages."

A wicked grin slides over his too-handsome face. "You like looking at a lot of things."

My stomach quivers in trepidation, like I'm slowly climbing toward that first drop of a roller coaster and it knows it's about to be left behind as the rest of my body plummets to the earth. "What's that supposed to mean?"

"Nothing yet." He pulls his phone from his pocket and thumbs over the screen a few times, then music starts playing through the small but powerful speaker he'd brought. Trey Songz's "Neighbors Know My Name"—a slow, sexy song about fucking his girl so well she can't stop screaming his name (I swear, the man is trying to kill me with innuendo)—fills the space of my little apartment. "Keep your eyes on me, Jane. I'm gonna give you a lot more to look at."

His hips start to sway from side to side, mesmerizing me like he's a snake charmer and I'm the idiot snake who can't tear my gaze away. Large hands skate over the front of his body, from his chest all the way down to where the hem of his white, ribbed tank is bunched at his waist. One thumb hooks under the shirt and slowly lifts it up as the other hooks into the band of his underwear and tugs the front down low.

Chance pulls the bottom of his shirt over and behind his head, anchoring it at the back of his neck so it looks like one of those gun harnesses you see cops wear. I find it oddly sexy that he doesn't take it completely off. Don't ask me why. It's not like it's covering anything up or leaving parts of him to the imagination.

Everything his torso has to offer is now on full display for my viewing pleasure. Things like his eight-pack of abs (ten, if you count the two obliques that slash into that delicious V) and the short, dark blond hair that flows over his pecs to meet in the middle, then continues as a thin trail that bisects the aforementioned glorious abs and picks back up beneath his naval to lead straight to the promised land. Halle-frickinglujah.

His body continues to undulate and move in ways much too fluid for someone with as much muscle mass as he has. It's sexy and erotic, like he's making love to the air, and for the first time in my life, I know what it's like to be struck dumb. I couldn't answer the simplest of questions right now if my life depended on it, so it's a damn good thing that it doesn't.

"Touch me, Jane."

His words snap me out of my stupor, and I close my mouth, which I only now realize has been hanging open like a boy seeing his first pair of tits. Could I *be* more pathetic? *Come on, Janey, toughen up!* I meet his gaze and attempt to appear bored. I arch a brow and say, "No thanks, I'm good."

"Mmmm," he hums while dragging his bottom lip through his teeth. "I'm betting you're better than good, Jane." Grabbing my hips, he drags me out of my corner to the center of the couch then braces his hands on the back of it, on either side of my head. He bends his arms like he's doing a pushup, bringing his upper body in close, and speaks directly into my ear. "I'm betting you're actually very, *very* bad."

All the air is pushed from my lungs. I let my head drop to rest on the back of the couch as he nuzzles my neck, bathing my skin with his warm breath. My breasts grow heavy, and my nipples tighten. "I don't know what you're talking about."

I almost sound drunk, but two glasses of wine aren't enough for that. No, it's not the fermented grapes making my speech lazy and slow. I've got a full-on buzz from too much Stripper Pale Ale.

He chuckles and pulls back far enough to look me in the eyes as he yanks my ass to the edge of the couch and spreads my legs apart. "Oh, I think you do, Jane. That's okay, though. You hold on to your facade as long as you can. It'll make it all the sweeter when I bare the real you."

"You're delusional." Except that he's not. He's actually

dead-fucking-on and I don't know how it's possible. It's one thing to be able to read people—and I have no doubt that in his profession he's gotten quite good at it—but it's quite another for him to look into my eyes like he can see all my filthy secrets. "I'm not baring anything to you. This is only a dance, remember?"

"It is," he says, "until you tell me it isn't."

"Cryptic much?"

His only response is a smug grin as he places his hands on either side of me, shoots his feet back, and drops on a downbeat in the music. I gasp when he buries his face against my sex, then undulates his body rhythmically with the bass as he slowly works his way back up. He makes sure to drag every part of his body through my legs, just barely grazing me—and yet it's like he's pressing me into the cushions as intimate as it feels.

Once again, he's back in his power position, hovering above me and grinding his pelvis against mine, mimicking the act of fucking me right here in my living room. The thin material of his coveralls might as well be gauze from the way I can feel what they're covering, and *Sweet Mother of God, the man is hard as a rock*.

I don't even know how to process that. My limited knowledge about strippers is that they never get even remotely stiff. Something about being sexually desensitized in their work environment—like how gynecologists aren't sporting raging boners from looking at a dozen vaginas every day. But for whatever reason, Chance's "sensitivity" is off the charts.

He holds my gaze with those fuck-me eyes, and it's getting harder and harder not to tear the rest of his clothes off and do exactly as those deep blue pools are suggesting. Without warning, he hooks his arms under my thighs and stands, lifting me up in one smooth motion so I'm on sitting on his shoulders. Normally a very innocent position to be in—I've played many a round of chicken fights in my parents' pool growing up—except I'm facing the *wrong damn way*. I let out a surprised squeal and grab on to his head, since it's buried between my legs and the only thing I have within reach at this height.

I don't hear his growl as much as I feel it penetrate my yoga pants and panties and vibrate over my sex. A tiny moan escapes me before I can stop it, and my fingers clench in his long hair. Chance does an about-face and carefully slides me down his body, but as soon as my feet touch the floor, he spins me around and presses a hand between my shoulder blades.

"That's it, baby," he says, pushing me down until my hands are braced on the coffee table. "Bend over and let me get at this ass."

My stomach quivers in delicious anticipation despite a tiny voice in my head telling me to put a stop to this madness. I open my mouth to voice a weak protest, but he drives his fingers beneath the loose bun at the back of my head and kneads my scalp. Tingles race down my spine as my eyelids drift closed on a groan. Suddenly his hand closes, grabbing on to a hank of my hair, and pulls. I draw in a swift breath as my neck and back arch, sticking my butt higher into the air.

I barely have enough time to process the jolt of apprehension that spears through me. I hear the *crack* a split second before stinging heat registers on my right ass cheek, and I cry out in utter shock.

Oh my God, he spanked me.

This is where Public Jane becomes outraged and asks him who the hell he thinks he is, smacking my ass like he owns it. Except she's being bound and gagged and tossed in a closet by Secret Jane, whose system is flooded with endorphins and whose panties are now soaked from the rough handling. And the traitorous bitch wants more.

"You liked that," he says as he starts to dry-hump me doggy style to the beat of the song. If it weren't for our clothes, his dick would be sliding in and out of me with the strength of his gyrations. As it is, his hard length is rubbing along my crease, creating fresh waves of wet heat from the friction and pressure. It's so distracting I almost forget to deny his claim.

"N-no, I didn't." *Yes, I did.*

Chance yanks back on my head until my body is flush with his, and he speaks directly against my ear. "You can't lie to me, Jane. I know your secret."

Panic seizes my chest. "What secret?"

He licks the outer shell of my ear. His breath fans the side of my face, and I break out in goose bumps. Then he whispers, "I saw the porn videos on your laptop."

I gasp, indignation bubbling to the surface at the invasion of my privacy. I try to turn around to distance myself from him and maybe even give him a slap for good measure, but he holds me to him with one arm banded over my ribs, and claps his free hand over my mouth. "Shhhhhh," he says, soothing my ruffled feathers with his voice and the brush of his fingers over a cotton-clad nipple. "Turn your brain off, sweetness. Listen to what your body is telling you it wants."

He moves his hands lower as he rolls our bodies side to side with the music like a scene out of *Dirty Dancing*. My head falls back on his shoulder. I inhale slowly and take in his scent, a combination of soap and hot pavement that reminds me of summertime in the city. I feel fingers graze over my sex, making it throb in time with my quickening pulse.

Little by little, the tension leaves my body, and I give in to the snake charmer once more.

"That's it, baby, feel the music," he says, encouragingly. "I wanna fuck you, Jane." A hand comes up to encircle my throat possessively as his other one cups my pussy and squeezes. A whimper escapes my lips, and I'm wracked with a shudder of pure need that takes me by surprise. "I wanna fuck you rough and hard like I know you want. Just like in your videos. I can do that for you, Jane. Would you like that?"

I imagine him doing the nasty things I've fantasized about but could never voice aloud. Things that even now I'm ashamed to admit in my own mind. A tremor of lust rolls through me, and I mewl into his palm as my hips instinctively push back against his hard cock. Chance growls and grinds against my ass, matching my enthusiasm.

"Fuck, yeah, Jane, just like that."

The hand over my mouth adjusts to grip my jaw as the other one drops down to cup my mound. His fingers cleave my pussy lips through my yoga pants. I'm so sensitive, like the years of inferior, mechanically-induced orgasms have screwed with my sensors, and now, experiencing a man's touch—and by man, I mean "sex god who's promising to make my wildest fantasies come true"—has me ready to explode within seconds. With the friction between my slick folds, the glancing pass over my clit makes me involuntarily jerk, but he holds me firmly in place.

"I want to use your body for my pleasure," he continues, "and watch you get pleasure from being used. Because you would, wouldn't you, Jane? You'd get off on being my fucking slut for the night."

Holy shit, my knees actually buckle when he says the word slut. I've always known how depraved I am in theory, but there's always been a part of me that wonders if I'll be turned on when actually faced with the same things I troll for on the porn sites. *Guess that answers* that *question.*

"Forget about what you think is right, and focus on what *feels* right. Embrace your darkest desires. There's no shame in what you want."

Shameless… What would it be like to let go like that? To not worry about what others might think and just…*be.*

Chance nips at my earlobe, the quick pinch dragging me from my thoughts. "Tell me what you want, Jane. Do you want to be my little slut for the night? Do you want me to fuck you like the bad girl I know you are?"

My mind reels, trying to keep up with the visceral reactions his words are having on me, but it's a lost cause. Every time he speaks, he sets fire to all the reasons my brain erects as to why this isn't a good idea, until all that's left is wanton desire—desire for all the things his words and his body are promising.

So, I let go of every inhibition I've ever had, embrace the drunken lust…and I nod.

Chapter Six

"Good answer," he growls and spins me to face him. He fists my hair and yanks my head back again while the fingers of his other hand stroke down the arch of my neck. "Do you know how to deep-throat a cock, Jane?"

My insides tremble at the thought of him taking my mouth and fucking my throat. "Yes."

"Of course you do," he says. "Every good slut knows how to properly suck cock."

His dark blue eyes hold my gaze captive as his hands trail down my sides and then gather my wrists together behind my back. Slowly, he drags the zipper of my hoodie down, the backs of his knuckles burning a trail over the center line of my body, then shoves the sides off my shoulders, exposing my breasts.

My breaths are little more than tiny, excited huffs, causing my wanton chest to rise and fall, beckoning him to look, to take notice of what I'm offering up to him. Or, more accurately, what I'm allowing him to take.

Finally, he tears his eyes away from mine so they can take their fill of what he's uncovered.

"No T-shirt, no bra," he muses. He squeezes one breast roughly, causing me to inhale sharply. "Were you hoping that your handyman would notice, Jane? Did you want him to see your hard nipples through the cotton of your sweatshirt? Did you want him to take advantage of you?"

The way he's kneading my breasts and pinching my nipples has me reeling, and I almost don't manage an answer, but at last I shake my head. "No," I say on a gasp when he tweaks one bud especially hard. "I wasn't hoping that."

"And how about now, Jane," he asks gruffly. "Now that you know *I'm* your handyman. A man with a hard body and even harder cock. A man who can fuck you better than any of the limp-dick pussies in your past. A man who can show you what it's like to be used so well your body will still be feeling me in a week."

I tremble. "Yes."

"Good girl. Now, get naked so I can see what's mine."

What's mine. What would it be like to have a domineering man like Chance claim me as his, even for a little while? I'm about to find out. It seems so surreal, this whole situation. It all happened so fast, from ordinary handyman to seductive stripper to unexpected lover. Though, that makes it sound too tender. What he is, is a fucker, and he's promising to be a better fuck than I've ever had.

He doesn't know that my lackluster sexual experiences thus far make his statement insignificant, but I think he has the potential to be better than my *future* experiences, and that fact leaves me both exhilarated and mildly depressed.

He steps back to give me room, and I suppose to give himself a better vantage point from which to watch. When I don't immediately move to follow his command, he crosses his arms and arches a brow in challenge.

This is the defining moment. If I want to change my mind, the time to do it is now, before I take the rest of my clothes off. But even though I can still, just barely, hear the rational voice telling me to come to my senses...I don't want to. I want this. I want *him*. All I have to do is be bold enough.

"Jane." His voice is a whip cracking in the air between us, spurring me into action.

Be bold enough, Janey. Taking a deep breath, I pull my arms from the sleeves and drop the hoodie behind me, then hook my thumbs into the waistband of my panties and drag them, and my yoga pants, down my legs before stepping out of them and removing my socks. I straighten to stand in front of Chance completely nude with the exception of the trim thatch of hair on my mound. I'm not the most confident woman—as evidenced by my steadily increasing anxiety the longer I'm not distracted by his heady touches—but I force my clenched hands to stay at my sides, and I wait.

His eyes roam heavily over my body, blazing a fiery path and making my skin feel tight and hot. Finally, his tank finds its way to the floor, leaving his upper body gloriously bare for my eyes to do a little roaming of their own. I assumed he'd take the rest of his clothes off, but he doesn't, making me feel more vulnerable than if he were naked with me.

I'm transfixed as he pulls his cock out from the constriction of his briefs and begins stroking himself. I know this is cliché, but sweet baby Jesus, the man is *huge*. Thick and long and hard as granite, with throbbing veins and a dusky head leaking clear drops of pre-cum I'm suddenly desperate to taste.

"You want my cock, Jane?" Wide eyed and transfixed, I nod. He walks backward until he's leaning against the wall with his feet spread apart, still lazily stroking himself from root to head and back again. "Then get on the floor and crawl for it, little slut."

I hesitate. My natural reaction is to war against the derogatory term and demeaning order. But at the same time, something inside me responds like it's being coaxed out from the cave and Chance is the sun, offering me his warmth and light. This might not be a conventional desire, but it is *mine*, and now that I've had a glimpse of what it's like outside of that cave, I don't want to go back.

Folding into myself, I get down on all fours. The Berber carpet is hard and scratchy under my hands and knees as I crawl—an apt reminder that my comfort is of no consequence to the man making the demands. I don't stop until I'm directly in front of him, my face mere inches from the gargantuan rod I now crave more than my next breath. Unfortunately, he doesn't seem to be in any rush to give it to me.

Peering up at him from beneath my lashes, I do what I suspect he wants: I beg. "Please, may I put your cock in my mouth?"

His full lips twist into a wicked grin. "Such lovely manners," he says. "I suppose I should reward you. Scoot in close then sit back on your heels. Shoulders back so I get a good look at those perky tits. That's it. Now, stick out your tongue."

I watch as he fists his hard shaft and guides the bulbous head to my open mouth. He drags the seeping tip over my flattened tongue, and the sweet taste of his pre-cum is like liquid candy. My mouth fills with saliva, greedy to taste more of him. Before I can rein myself in, I close my lips around him and suck for all I'm worth, trying to milk whatever his cock will give me as I tongue its tiny slit.

I hear Chance hiss in a breath and growl out, "*Fuck*," before a hand fists in the back of my hair and yanks me away. His free hand grabs my jaw hard enough to hurt, but not so hard that he'll leave bruises. As he leans over me, I'm forced to meet his angry gaze, and a bolt of apprehension shoots through me. I don't know this man. I don't know if he has a mean streak a mile wide and a rap sheet to prove it. What the hell am I doing? This could be my worst best decision ever, and if it turns out I'm really dancing with the devil, it could be the last decision I ever make.

"Though I'll admit the feel of those lips sucking at my dick like a goddamn Hoover was pretty fucking amazing, that's not what I told you to do, is it?"

I stare into his deep blue eyes and search for signs of malice or ill intent. Signs that I should lock myself in my room and call 911. But I don't see anything like that. Instead, all I see are flames of desire that match mine, that are licking at both of us and pushing us to give in to the consummation of the ultimate pleasure.

"You still good, Jane?"

The tone of his question hints at the civil man who fixed my sink in exchange for a dance. He's checking in with me, and I'm certain that if I answer no, everything will come to a stop. Playtime with Chance will be over, and I'll never know what it's like to have this kind of freedom with a lover who truly understands what I want.

Any remaining shreds of trepidation dissipate into the ether, and what's left behind is a burning need for this man to control me, to use me…to fuck me.

An impish grin lifts the corners of my mouth, and I toss down the verbal gauntlet I hope will unleash the animal I can see straining at its tether inside him.

"Do your worst."

Chapter Seven

Chance

Do my worst? Fuuuuck *me*. It must be my birthday because this woman is the best kind of present. Meek and obedient one minute, wicked and insubordinate the next. Part angel, part devil, and all mine. At least for now, which is fine because that's all I'm interested in.

I chuckle, outwardly mocking her bravery even as I secretly praise her for it.

"My worst?" I repeat. "A little thing like you couldn't handle my worst. But don't you worry. There's still plenty I *can* give you. Open your mouth."

I'm still gripping her jaw, so she doesn't have much choice, but she opens wide anyway. She's eager for my cock. Her little stunt a few seconds ago confirmed that, and I'm more than happy to give it to her.

I release my hold on her jaw and guide the fat head of my dick past those pouty lips. The wet heat of her mouth makes me hiss in a breath. I steadily push my hips forward, demanding she take more of me. I'm bigger than average — a fact I'm reminded of every time a woman sees my cock for the first time — but I want to see how far I can push Jane. How much of me she'll take before tapping out.

Her brown eyes, glassy and dark with desire, start to water as I hit the back of her throat. She's taking quick puffs of air through her nose, but she's not ready to take me deeper yet. Reluctantly, I pull out and watch with satisfaction as strings of her spit keep us connected. She drags in deep gulps of air, her perky tits heaving. "Good," I growl. "Again."

This time I don't go slow. Orientation is over. I use my thumb to press my cock down to line up with her open mouth and drive forward until she gags, then pull back out. I do it again and again, reveling in the way she looks on her knees for me, and the sounds she makes every time I retreat and let her take a quick breath.

Her eyelashes are spiked with the wetness of her eyes watering. If I weren't an expert in reading women, I might think the tears streaming down her temples to disappear into her hairline are ones of distress. But I'm paying attention to those beautiful pools of dark chocolate, and they're telling me that Jane is loving every minute of this.

She's driving me fucking insane. I've been sucked off by hundreds of women — yes, hundreds — and something about Jane is making this feel different, better. It's gotta be because for the first time ever, a woman isn't fawning over me or actively trying to be the next one to ride my dick. There's no other explanation. A hole is a hole — it all feels the same to a guy. Sure there are some techniques that might make certain things better, but give a guy a warm, wet hole with some friction, and he's gonna blow his load, guaranteed. We're easy as shit like that.

So I refuse to think that the reason Jane Wendall is blowing my mind right now is for any other reason than it's a turn-on to fuck her when she was so against even getting a dance in the beginning.

"Deeper now, baby. Open that throat," I say as I start pushing past that natural barrier. I adjust my position so my booted feet are planted on either side of her. Then I hold her head with both hands and start fucking her the way I want to fuck her pussy.

I groan as I slide fully inside of her. The minx wasn't kidding. She's deep-throating me like a goddamn porn star, and I can't help but wonder if she learned how from all the kinky videos she watches. I've never been so grateful porn exists than I am in this moment.

She reaches up and gently squeezes my balls, and I almost blow right fucking then. "Jesus Christ," I say through gritted teeth as I yank back. We're both breathing hard as hell, but I'm doing my damnedest to get myself under control. "You wanna play, baby? Let's play."

I pull her up and set her on the arm of the couch, pushing her end table out of the way with my foot to give me more room to maneuver. I shove my coveralls and boxer briefs down past my ass, but not before I grab a condom from the back pocket and sheath myself in record time. I want inside this woman so bad I can't fucking think.

Placing my hand in the center of her chest, I push until she's angled back with only her shoulder blades braced against the back of the couch, then roughly shove her legs apart. "Hold them up, just like this." I show her how to hook her arms under her knees and give me access to everything I want. She complies, and I stare at her glistening pussy, pink and swollen and slick with her juices. Fuck me, I don't think I've seen a prettier cunt.

"Please, Chance," she pleads. "I want to come. Make me come."

I give her a light slap right on her pussy. She jumps and

cries out, then again when I pinch each of her nipples between my thumbs and forefingers. "You don't get to decide what I do and don't do, Jane. Do you?" I ask with a little twist.

Her back arches on another cry, and the words "I'm sorry" tumble from her lips over and over. I release her nipples and lean forward, one hand bracing against the couch and the other gripping her jaw to force her to meet my steely gaze. "You're not sorry yet, Jane, but you will be. You want to come so bad? I'm gonna make you come until you can't handle it anymore. Until you're begging me to stop."

She bites her lower lip, teeth sinking into her plump flesh. It takes every ounce of control I have not to claim her lip for myself and suck on it like a piece of hard candy. I have a feeling I'd lose my focus and start exploring her in ways that don't fit this particular script. And I'm really liking this script.

Standing straight again, I strum her clit, fast and furious, and watch her as she chases her orgasm. Her moans and whimpers make me hard to the point of pain, my balls like heavy stones ready to explode, but I grit my teeth and force myself to hold out.

Sweat makes her skin glow; her breaths steadily get shorter. It takes less than thirty seconds for her to fall the first time. Her jaw drops open on a silent scream, her climax momentarily cutting off her ability to draw in air or make a single sound. Those brown eyes I find so captivating briefly roll back, showing me only the whites, like a woman possessed, and I know it's not far from the truth. It's a thing of fucking beauty, and I want to see more of it.

"Again," I command and immediately start rubbing her clit. A tiny squeal of surprise escapes her, and she impulsively tries to push my hand away. "Oh, I don't think so." I throw her hands back and give her another slap on her sex.

Jane yelps and pouts at me, but I can see the playfulness dancing in her eyes. She's loving this every bit as much as I am.

I hold her legs with one arm and push them back to expose more of her ass. Then I let my free hand fly. Alternating cheeks, I spank her, turning that flawless complexion a dusky red. Her curses, muttered through clenched teeth and full-body flinches, have melted into soft moans and obedient stillness. It fills me with satisfaction and a strange sense of pride to watch her react so beautifully. I get the feeling she doesn't have much experience, if any, with her particular brand of kink, and though I'm not getting too extreme, I'm not taking it easy on her either.

Her eyes are almost black, lids at half-mast as she stares up at me with a look of unabashed hunger. Unable to prolong our mutual pleasure any longer, I end her punishment and arrange her into the original position.

"You move," I say, "or try to stop me again, and I'll make you wish you hadn't. Understand?"

She nods in urgency. "Please. I'll be good."

I answer with a grunt that says *I'll be the judge of that*. "And if you're good, what is it you think I should give you as a reward?"

"Your cock," she says without hesitation. "I want you to fuck me. Hard and deep."

Fuck, she's killing me. Abso-fucking-lutely killing me. I fist my cock and slide it through her soaking pussy lips, teasing her clit with my sensitive head. It's utter torture, but I refuse to let her know that. As far as she's concerned, I can do this all damn day. Her hips writhe, and I know she's trying to get me to slip inside her. I slap her inner thigh and tell her to hold still.

"You want me to use your body as my little fuck hole? To fuck you so hard you'll feel me every time you touch your pussy for the next week and wish I was here to do it all over again?"

"Yes," she says on a breathy moan.

"Good answer." With that, I line myself up and shove balls deep inside of her.

I think my vision actually winks out for a couple of seconds. Jane's so tight and hot. Her sweet cunt is gripping me like her life depends on it, and I'm not entirely sure that mine doesn't. She rocks her hips, needing me to move, but I need her stone still or I'm going to blow like a kid with his first titty mag.

That's when her inner walls squeeze my cock. *Fuck it.* I withdraw almost completely before thrusting in to the hilt. I groan, but I doubt she hears it over the shout she lets out as she throws her head back. I get a firm grip on her hips, digging my fingers into her soft flesh, and hold her in place as I use my cock like a battering ram. She's stretched around me—there isn't a place in her I'm not filling. I can feel it.

The musky scent of our arousal mixes with the sweat covering our bodies, and the floral scent of her shampoo invades my nose and turns me on that much more. Jane wraps her arms around my neck for support, and I press my forehead against hers. I hold her gaze as I fuck her brains out. It doesn't matter that I'm the one in the dominant role here. This woman is fucking me like mad just by the way she looks at me; the way she begs me to go faster, deeper, harder.

I clench my jaw and try to hold out, but the frisson of electricity shoots down my spine and settles in my balls.

I slip one hand between our bodies. I press my fingers into her lower abdomen, just above her pubic bone, helping the friction from my cock stimulate her g-spot as my thumb flicks over her clit. She moans and tosses her head back as her legs start to tremble around my waist.

"Look at me," I rasp, my breath coming quick and harsh. She does, her face flushed and her pupils blown out in pleasure.

"Oh, God, Chance, I can't," she whimpers. "It's *too much*."

"Yes, you fucking can. Let go with me, Jane. I want you to come on my cock. Let me feel your sweet cunt milking me dry." She's close, *so fucking close*. All she needs is something to tip that scale…

Maybe another small taste of humiliation. "*Now*, goddamn it, or I'll drag you out into the hall for everyone to watch as I slap your pussy until you come, just like the little slut you are."

"Oh, *fuuuuuuuck*!" she screams as her orgasm washes over her, and mine is right on her heels.

White-hot lightning shoots through my entire body as I empty myself inside her with every thrust. Her pussy is convulsing around me, trying to suck me back in each time I retreat. It doesn't have to worry, though, because I can't think of a place I'd rather be than buried inside Jane.

After what seems like an eternity, and yet not long enough, I pull completely out and set her on the couch. She covers up with a throw blanket, and I make a quick pit stop in her bathroom to dispose of the condom, and I redress as I try to process the last hour.

I've never had such dirty sex with such a clean girl before. And that's what Jane is—a clean girl. I don't mean in the hygienic sense, or that she's naively innocent—her internet porn collection pretty much nixes that label. It's gonna sound cheesy as hell, but it's more like…her soul.

There, I said it. Her soul is clean. Or maybe pure is a better word. Yeah, her soul is pure.

Jane didn't just let me fuck her. She gave herself over to me, no questions asked. She didn't know me from Adam, yet she trusted me not to hurt her despite the entire setup being the kind of sex where the intention is to use her body and use it roughly.

Goddamn it, she shouldn't have trusted me. What the hell was she thinking? I could've been a sick fuck with a twisted agenda. We didn't even discuss safe words. I've never used them before, but I've never before fucked anyone with that kind of power exchange. Sure, I've had a ton of rough sex—it's my preferred brand—but the woman is usually just as rough, giving as much as she's getting.

What I did with Jane was different. She laid herself bare and made herself vulnerable to me. For me. And it's fucking with my mind, because all I can think about is taking her into her bedroom for a marathon of sex followed by a mini-coma. That's how I know my shit is scrambled. I've never spent the night at a client's place, no matter how many bonus dances we had. When we were done, I always packed up and went home.

Tonight would be no different. Jane Wendall isn't special, and I need to make that known before she invites me to stay over and offers to make blueberry pancakes in the morning. Decision made, I stride back into the living room to find an equally clothed Jane, and berate myself for being disappointed I can't see her naked one more time before I leave.

Fucking get yourself together, Danvers.

"Your membership to that site definitely paid off. You fuck like a porn star. I'd even go so far as to say you've made my Top Ten list. Congratulations," I say, a smug smirk firmly in place.

Jane blinks up at me, and her jaw falls slack. The look of hurt that flickers across her face makes me feel like a Grade A asshole, but I need to stick to my guns. This—like all my other "bonus dances"—is a one-off. It's better if she feels the same way, and a sure bet of making that happen is to make it so she never wants to see me again.

"I think it's time for you to go."

She walks over to the door and pulls it open, staring at me expectantly. *Mission accomplished.* I gather my toolbox and head toward her. On my way out, I notice a royal blue IHOP apron draped over one of the dining chairs. With deduction skills that would make Sherlock envious, I figure she must work at one of the many breakfast restaurant locations. Though I tell it not to, my brain files that info away for another time.

As I walk past her, she says stiffly, "Thank you for fixing my broken pipe."

I step into the hall and turn to face her. "If anything else needs fixing," I say, making my quick perusal of her body obvious and driving that final nail into my coffin, "you have my number."

She huffs, narrowing her eyes. "Don't hold your breath." Then she slams the door in my face, which is exactly what I deserve.

Chapter Eight

CHANCE

"Why the hell do you keep dragging us here, Chance? This shit's gonna give me a spare tire."

I glance up from the menu I'm pretending to scan, and look at one of my best friends and business partners, Austin Massey. "Then stop ordering the pancakes, dumbass. Get an egg white omelet and quit your bitchin'."

Austin makes a face like I just suggested he eat plastic. "You can't come to the International House of Pancakes and not get pancakes. It's sacrilege, or at the very least, a universal law."

Looking for some help in giving our friend shit for worrying about his calorie intake, I turn my attention to the man sitting in the corner of the booth next to Austin. But as usual, Roman Reeves is typing furiously on his phone, probably sending an email or instructions to his assistant about some case or another. The term "off duty" doesn't exist in his vocab. It's five in the fucking morning, and Roman has already worked out, juiced his own breakfast, and dressed in a charcoal gray Armani suit. Dude runs his life on a tighter schedule than the president.

Not for the first time, I muse at how different we've all become since our partying days at UW Madison.

"Roman," I say, slapping the table in front of him. "You gonna look up from that thing and weigh in on this conversation, or what?"

He keeps his eyes on his phone and his fingers moving over the keyboard. "You mean the one where Massey is whining about ruining his girlish figure?" It always amazes me how he manages to do ten things at once like that. I do my best work when I focus intently on one task — or one woman — at a time. Then once I'm done, I move on to something else.

Austin lowers his menu. "Hey, how 'bout you guys bite me."

"That's the one, yeah," I say, ignoring Austin.

Finished with whatever he was doing, Roman locks his screen and sets his phone down where he can see if notifications come through. "I'd rather discuss the question you've evaded from the beginning. Why do you keep telling us to meet you at IHOP? Three times in one weekend and now this morning? What's the deal, Danvers?"

"You got a problem with IHOP all of a sudden? We haven't seen a lot of each other lately. Excuse me for wanting to see my friends and get some food at the same time."

The lie tastes bitter, and I take a drink of my ice water to try and wash it down. I have no idea what I'm fucking doing. Correction. I know exactly what I'm doing. I just have no clue *why* I'm doing it, or why I'm not being straight with the guys. It's not like they won't see what's up as soon as she comes over to the table.

I'd gotten shit for sleep on Friday after leaving Jane's place. I kept reliving the way she'd looked and felt and tasted.

I don't know what it is, but something makes her different from the countless women I've hooked up with before, and I haven't been able to get her out of my mind. After a sleepless night, I convinced myself that if the sex was that fucking good—and it was—then there's nothing wrong with wanting a repeat performance.

But with the spectacular way I left things between us, I'd known there was zero chance she'd give me the time of day if I showed up at her apartment, which had sparked the idea of showing up at her work. I figured she wouldn't be able to outright dismiss me if I'm a paying customer, and the likelihood of her causing a scene will hopefully be low. She doesn't strike me as the drama-queen type.

Before I could think better of it, I started making calls to all the IHOP's in the area, asking when Jane Wendall's next shift was. The first two I called responded by saying no one by that name worked there. But the third one said they couldn't give me that information. *Bingo.*

After that, all I had to do was drop a couple hundred dollars taking my buddies to breakfast, dinner, lunch, and now breakfast again. It was only a matter of time before we visited during one of her shifts, and in this case, the fourth time is a charm.

I flick my gaze over to the waitress station where Jane is entering in an order. Watching her, knowing she has no idea I'm here, is kind of a turn-on. Her long chestnut hair is in a ponytail, and it swings behind her, the ends brushing her shoulder blades, as she chats with another waitress. I want to wrap it around my hand and pull back so her neck is arched for me again. So I can suck on it and bite it and hear her gasps turn into moans, just like the other night.

Christ, my cock reacts to her as easily as it did to a stiff wind when I was thirteen. If I don't get myself under control, I'm going to need my menu to hide the pocket rocket straining against the fly of my jeans.

Jane collects a coffee carafe and makes her way over to us while shoving a handful of straws in the front of her apron. She has yet to look up, navigating the aisles by heart, her strides quick and efficient, and yet my brain sees her naked and exaggerating the swing of her hips like a woman approaches her man in the bedroom. Fuck me. My mind and body have both gone rogue.

When she reaches us, she sets the carafe on the table, pulls out her order pad, and makes eye contact with Austin and Roman first. She pushes her glasses up higher and smiles. "Good morning, gentlemen. What can I—" Her smile falters, and her eyes widen when they finally land on me. "You," she whispers. "What are you doing here?"

Her face flushes, and her gaze darts around like she's suddenly worried the entire restaurant can tell what we did on Friday. That's impossible, of course, but it won't be long before my friends put two and two together and come up with "bonus dance." Maybe I should have told them the truth, but I'm not even sure what the truth is. Either way, it's too late now.

I give her my best wicked grin and say, "Why, Jane, fancy meeting you here. I came in for some breakfast with my friends before we head off to work."

Her forehead furrows, putting the most adorable crinkle above her nose as she glances around the table once again, taking in my friends' various wardrobe choices. Roman's suit, Austin's navy blue Dickies with a T-shirt proclaiming "I became a firefighter for the money and fame," and my worn jeans with holes in the knees and my Danvers & Son Construction T-shirt. We'd make a great joke. *So, a handyman, a businessman, and a fireman all walk into an IHOP…*

Jane is definitely confused. "You mean you're just now getting *off* of work?"

Roman arches a dark brow in my direction while Austin
turns his pretty-boy charms on Jane, smiling at her like she's
the new toy in the playroom. If he's not careful, he'll be
picking his teeth up from the faded blue carpet. "She thinks
we just got done entertaining a group of ladies," I explain.
"Right, Jane?"

"Yes. I mean, no…um…"

Roman grins in her direction. "Not many parties happen
on a Sunday night, beautiful. Besides," he says, his grin turning
sharkish, "we'd look a lot less put-together if we'd just come
from getting mauled by a group of horny women, don't you
think?"

That's Roman for you. He's the epitome of an upstanding
gentleman…until he's not. His nickname is Ruthless, and it
applies in every aspect of his life, whether with work or with
women.

Austin, the smooth operator that he is, jumps in to save
her. "You'll have to forgive my friends. They've never known
how to act when a lady's present." Austin lived the first fifteen
years of his life in Texas before moving to Chicago. He lost
most of his accent over the years, but likes to use the country
boy act around women because that shit works.

He takes one of her hands and kisses the back of it. It's
everything I have not to kick him in the balls under the table
for daring to touch her. Which makes no fucking sense. I've
shared plenty of women with these guys. It's hot as fuck, and
we all enjoy it. I should be encouraging his usual seduction,
seeing how she responds, and gauging our odds of tag-teaming
her later.

So why do I want to rip her hand from Massey's and
growl *mine* like a goddamn caveman?

"To alleviate your confusion, darlin', we all have day jobs."
Austin winks and leans a little closer before whispering, "We
do the strippin' for fun."

"Oh," she says, finally pulling her hand away. She blinks as though waking up from a spell, which if you ask him, is exactly what Austin calls his Southern charm.

"Um…" Jane shakes her head and poises her pen over the order pad. "What can I get you this morning?"

She avoids me, giving her attention to the guys, and I can't decide whether it pisses me off or amuses me. Since the jig is up, and my buddies now know why we've been coming here for going on three days, they look at me. Roman says, "You wanted something specific, didn't you, Chance?"

"Yeah," I say, picking up the menu. "But I don't see it on here."

Jane moves closer to look at the plastic pages with me. "Oh, we just got new menus. What is it you want?"

I turn my head, my mouth inches away from her face. "You."

She freezes for a moment then abruptly straightens. The guys are chuckling under their breath. I don't go quite that far, instead giving her a sly grin as I undress her with my eyes. That blue polo doesn't do a damn thing to show off her slight figure, but I don't need it to because I know exactly what her pert tits look like.

Color flags her cheekbones. She looks around to make sure no one is listening, then she braces her hands on the table and leans in, speaking softly. "Be serious. Do you want something to eat or not?"

I fold my arms over my forgotten menu and lean over to meet her the rest of the way. I don't give a shit who hears me, but she's like a planet to my moon, drawing me to her. I find myself wanting to be in her personal space as much as possible. To inhale her mouth-watering strawberry scent and make her nervous, set her on edge. "I'm being very serious. I'm hungry for you, Jane. So tell me what I have to do to get you on my menu."

Chapter Nine

JANE

I can't do this. I can't be near *him* without my body betraying me. I need to get a grip, get some air, get some fucking perspective. "Excuse me," I say to the three ridiculously gorgeous men at table nine, and make a beeline for the ladies' bathroom, bursting through the door as though the hounds of hell are nipping at my heels.

I brace my hands on the sink and stare at my reflection. My face is flushed from the things Chance said to me. I was so rattled that I didn't even remember to take my apron off, which violates the health code. Up until now, I've never forgotten to remove it before entering the restroom. My reaction pisses me off, which doesn't help matters. He shouldn't affect me like this. I mean, yeah, okay, the man is the sexiest thing I've ever laid eyes on. Even with a faded green T-shirt, holey jeans, and his hair pulled back into a short ponytail at his nape, he still manages to look Hollywood beautiful. And, apparently, his deep voice was now the trigger for my libido because as soon as he spoke, my panties became damp. I don't think it would matter if he innocently recited the entire menu. Everything he said would sound like a sexual innuendo.

Sure, he gave me the best sex of my life—better than I ever thought possible—but he'd ruined it by acting like a dick.

I'm not an idiot. I wasn't expecting, nor wanting, expressions of adoration or devotion. I wasn't planning to cling to his leg and beg him to stay. But it wouldn't have killed him to be a mature adult about it, either.

Top Ten list? Ha! As if I care.

It's not like I obsessed all weekend about *where* on that list I might be, or what the other girls who made the list were like, or how many girls he'd been with total (a hundred…two hundred… *five hundred*?) in his man-whorish life. Nope. Absolutely *zero* obsessing happened since he left my apartment Friday night.

I've also recently taken up the hobby of lying to myself profusely. *Ugh.*

"Maybe if I stay in here long enough," I say to myself in the mirror, "they'll just go away."

That actually doesn't sound like a half-bad plan. They're my only table, and all my prep work is done. If Sally comes looking for me, I'll say I don't feel well and ask her to cover for me. I can't really afford to lose this shift, especially after I took the weekend off to celebrate my mom's birthday with the family, but I'd rather eat Ramen noodles for the next week than go back out there and face Chance.

Decision made, I turn to go hibernate in one of the stalls when the door to the restroom flies open, scaring me half to death. Chance storms in, a scowl on his face as he grabs me by the arm and pulls me into the stall, and now my pulse is racing for a different reason entirely. He slides the lock home and then traps me between his arms against the metal door.

"Why do I get the feeling you're avoiding me, Jane?"

"Why do you say my name all the time?" I ask, hoping to

distract him from his own question. But I'm also genuinely curious. No one has ever said my name like he does.

"I like your name," he says, his deep blue eyes penetrating me. "I like the way it sounds, the way it feels when I say it."

"Me, too." Too late, I realize I said that aloud instead of in my head where I'd meant it to stay. Damn it, this man makes me crazy. Crazy mad, crazy turned on, and crazy frustrated. Every time he says my name, it makes my stomach turn inside out and my knees go weak. My parents nicknamed me Janey, and it's pretty much what everyone calls me, with the exception of my professors and other official-type people.

But when Chance says it, it sounds anything but professional. He makes it sound like a dirty command, one I want to obey with every cell in my body.

He smirks at my admission, which only serves to piss me off. "You can't be in here. You need to leave. In fact, you should *leave* leave, as in, the restaurant. I don't know what game you're playing, but I don't find it amusing in the least."

"I'll leave as soon as you agree to see me again."

My jaw drops as I try to process his words… Nope. It's not working. I must have misheard him. "I'm sorry, what?"

"You heard me. I told you before, I don't like repeating myself, Jane."

Yes, he did tell me before, and the memory of it causes a rush of warmth between my legs. "I don't understand. You want to date me?"

"No," he says, pressing the front of his body to mine so I can feel his erection before he speaks in my ear. "I want to fuck you."

For a split second, my gut twists at his immediate dismissal—like he'd never even *consider* dating me—but then my libido dropkicks my fragile ego and jumps in its place. *Yes! Fuck me, fuck me!* Wait, no, what am I thinking? This guy is *no bueno*. Bad Janey. Giving myself a mental smack upside the head, I gather all the bravado I can muster. "And what makes you think *I* want to fuck *you*?"

I draw in a sharp breath when he pulls my apron aside and dips down enough to grind his cock against my clit. "I've had your scent in my nose all goddamn weekend. I can smell your arousal, Jane, and I'd bet both of my companies that if I slide my hand into your khakis right now, you'd soak my fingers. Wouldn't you?"

Oh God, if he kept this up I'd be humping his leg like a dog. His words are fogging up my brain like the windows of a car at Lookout Point.

Hold on, what did he say about companies? "You own two companies?"

"Don't change the subject."

The door to the restroom opens, and we listen as a woman heads to the double vanity. I peek through the crack of the stall door and silently curse. It's Darla, another of my co-workers coming in for her shift. She's a single mom, and is always too tired to do her makeup before she takes the baby to daycare, so she does it in the bathroom before work. Darla puts some music on low from her phone and starts taking things out of her cosmetic bag.

I look at Chance, expecting to see an "oh shit" expression to match mine. Instead, he might as well have horns sprouting from his forehead to complement the devilish glint in his eyes and the wicked curve of his mouth. *He wouldn't dare...*

Oh, yes, he would. My stomach drops when his hand presses between my thighs and moves up to my sex. I push his hand away and shake my head, but he retaliates by pinning my wrists above my head with one large hand and then returns the other to where he'd had it.

He places his lips next to my ear and whispers so quietly that there's no way Darla can hear him. "I'm gonna make you come, sweetness. Right here, right now, with that woman only a few feet from us." Chance's deft fingers undo the button on my pants and slowly slide the zipper down. My breaths grow shallow. "She could catch us at any minute, peek under the stall to see what's going on if she hears something strange. So you have to be absolutely silent. Nod if you understand."

I shouldn't. I should wrench myself from his grip, shove him away, and get the hell out of here. I can think of something to tell Darla and everyone later, and hopefully Patrick, my asshole boss, won't fire me.

Just when I think I've worked up enough resolve to carry out my plan, he slips his hand into my panties. "Nod, Jane."

Game over. I nod.

"Good girl."

He pulls back and watches me as his fingers slip between the folds of my pussy, spreading my wetness from front to back. When his touch glances over my clit, my entire body jerks and my mouth opens, ready to betray me, but I bite my lip at the last damn second. He almost looks disappointed, and it wouldn't surprise me one bit if his goal is to get me to cry out as he finger-fucks me in a bathroom stall at my place of employment.

Well, I'll be damned if I'm going to give him that satisfaction. I focus on my body and try to get it back under control. I slow my breathing, taking deeper breaths through my nose to prevent myself from panting, and I force my muscles to relax.

Chance narrows his eyes at me, my resolve evidently a challenge to him. One he gladly accepts as he pushes two fingers so deep inside me that I rise up on my toes. He releases my wrists and my hands automatically fall to his powerful shoulders, my nails digging in for purchase through the soft cotton of his shirt.

He starts fucking me with his hand, pumping in and out, and if it weren't for Darla's music and my clothes muffling the sounds, she'd be able to hear the wet suction of my channel gripping his thick fingers. The band in my stomach starts to twist, signaling the beginning of my climax. My slow breathing is shot all to hell, and the smug look on his face confirms that he enjoys making me lose control.

As though proving my point, he does something I'm in no way prepared for and slips a well-lubricated finger into my ass. My eyes grow big in shock, and I forget all about being quiet. But Chance must have been ready for that because he claps his free hand over my mouth before any sound escapes. His wicked smile causes a shiver to race down my spine as he finger-bangs both of my holes while thumbing my clit.

My orgasm is so close, but just out of reach. I'm nervous that Darla's going to catch me with my pants down, quite literally, and it edges on panic when she turns off her playlist and starts packing up her things. What little bit of noise we're making—the air rushing in and out through my nose and the wet sound of my pussy—is too loud without the music to drown it out, so Chance switches tactics. He stops all motion in my pants with the exception of his thumb, but leaves his fingers buried all the way to his last knuckles, and the hand over my mouth moves to wrap around the front of my throat, squeezing on the sides just enough to slow the blood flow.

As the seconds tick by, my orgasm builds, the rubber band in my belly twisting more and more as the edges of my vision start to blur and my body begins to tremble. He looms over me, his huge frame consuming the tiny space, making me feel powerless and helpless and completely at his mercy…and I love it.

I crave his dominance and the abject humiliation he gives me, like an addict craves his next hit. Before experiencing sex with Chance, I'd often felt ashamed of what I wanted, of how I wanted to be treated by a partner. But when Chance has me in hand, I couldn't care less what's considered normal. This does it for me. *He* does it for me.

My face is damp with sweat. I'm so close, so fucking close. The muscles in his jaw are flexing, and his blue eyes are dark with lust. I can't breathe or think or feel anything beyond the full body orgasm bearing down on me, and I wonder if I'll actually pass out before I have it.

Darla turns the water on in the sink and lets it run. Chance takes advantage of the few precious seconds and fucks me fast and furious as he whispers a harsh command in my ear. "Come for me, Jane. *Now*."

He releases the hold on my throat, and the blood rushes to my head as I finally come with an explosive orgasm like I've never felt. He grabs the back of my head and pulls me into him, so I bite down on the thick cord in his neck to help stifle the scream that wants to escape. My entire body seizes and shakes at the same time, my pussy and ass convulsing over and over again, squeezing his fingers like a vise.

Darla turns the water off and dries her hands while Chance slowly pumps inside me, helping me ride out the last of my climax. When the restroom door squeals shut, I sag back against the stall and let my head drop back as I try to catch my breath. I whimper as he starts to pull out of me.

"Shhhhhh," he says with his cheek pressed at my temple, and his warm breath ruffles wisps of my hair. "You did so well, Jane. You were perfect." I swell with pride. His approval and compliments fill up a part of me untouched by anyone else.

Finally, he pulls back, leaving me feeling empty after he's no longer inside me. I hate it. Why does this man who's practically a stranger to me affect me so strongly on so many levels? Will I ever experience these things with someone else, or is he ruining me for—?

All thoughts grind to a halt as I watch him lick the two fingers he'd had buried in my sex with an expression of pure satisfaction on his handsome face. *Just when I think he can't be any sexier...*

As soon as he's done, it's like a switch goes off and he turns from Hot Sex Chance to All Business Chance. He zips and buttons my pants, straightens my apron, and then reaches around to grab my phone from my back pocket. I'm too dazed to ask him what he's doing, but after a few seconds, his phone starts to ring. He gets it out and shows me the screen lit up with my number.

"I added myself to your contacts, and now I can add you to mine," he says, replacing my phone in my pocket. "I'll give you a call, and we can do this again sometime."

The reminder of his earlier proposition finally snaps me out of my orgasmic brain fog. "Why me?" I demand coolly. "Did the other nine in your Top Ten list get sick of your assholish post-coitus comments?"

Chance winces the slightest bit and runs a hand over the back of his neck. Color me surprised—it appears he might actually feel guilty. But he doesn't let it show for more than a few seconds before regaining his unapologetic confidence.

"Okay, I deserve that," he concedes. "I'm sorry I acted like an asshole. To be honest, I don't have any kind of list, but sex with you the other night was…good."

I arch a brow at him because was he even in the same room as me the other night? That's the lamest adjective I can think of to describe what we did.

A hint of a smile ticks up one side of his mouth. "Fine, it was *really* good." *Smartass.* "Point is, I think we've got an opportunity here. Not everyone gets off on the things we do, but you and me, we're a match in the bedroom, Jane. Why not take advantage of it?"

Dear God, I want to say yes. Especially since I'm still coming down from the incredible orgasm *he* just gave me. His offer is so tempting…but not perfect. "I wouldn't mind having a casual, sex-only thing, but I'm not interested in being one in a flock of women you fuck, Chance. Call me old-fashioned, but I like to be at least *semi*-exclusive with my no-strings-sex."

"You drive a hard bargain, Jane." He narrows his eyes and crosses his arms over his chest. "All right, I'll agree that while we're fucking, I won't fuck anyone else. But then I have a concession of my own."

This is me, the cat, sniffing around the box clearly marked Curiosity. "Such as?"

"I want you bare."

Boom. Box explodes. "Bare," I repeat, swallowing thickly. "As in…"

"As in no condoms."

Briefly, I fantasize about how it would feel to have his thick length inside of me without a barrier, but I regain my senses before agreeing to anything stupid. "I'm sure that's not a problem for other women you entertain, but I'm not nearly as careless with my body."

Bracing a hand on the door above me, he leans in, making my bravado shrink along with the space separating us. "I'm not careless with anything. I always wear a rubber and get tested regularly. But if we're going to be exclusive for this, I don't see why we shouldn't take advantage of the situation. Are you on birth control?"

"Yes," I say slowly, a little ashamed of my rude assumption about his character.

"Good. Then we can trade test results and be done with it," he says, dipping his head to graze the side of my neck with his teeth. My breath shudders past my lips, and I have to lock my knees to keep myself standing. "I'll be able to take you whenever I want, with nothing in my way. Do we have a deal?"

Let's see, a safe, exclusive, no-strings arrangement with the sexiest man in the city who indulges my darkest fantasies? Sign. Me. Up. And yet, I don't immediately ask him to hand me a pen and point to the dotted line. This man is too cocky for his own good (no pun intended). It won't kill him if I make him sweat a little.

He pulls back to hear my answer. I cant my head, narrow my eyes a bit, and chew thoughtfully on the inside of my cheek. With each passing second, I see him getting more and more irritated. He's probably never had a girl contemplate—fake or not—anything involving him and sex. Poor thing. Guess I should put him out of his misery. "Deal."

He holds out his hand, and for a few seconds, I can only stare at it. The formal gesture makes me realize that we've never kissed. I wonder if he's against it a la *Pretty Woman*, because that would be a damn shame. Hoping that isn't the case, I put it in the back of my mind and shake his hand.

Chance grips me harder and pulls me in, his other hand smoothing over my ass and cupping my still swollen sex from behind, causing me to shudder with latent aftershocks. "Fair warning, baby. My sexual appetite is vast, and now you're all I have to stave off my hunger." He crushes his lips to mine, simultaneously banishing all worries of an anti-kissing agenda and revving me up for another round, consequences be damned. Sucking my bottom lip into his mouth, he gives it a sharp nip, then soothes it with his tongue.

Leaving me reeling, he pulls away and rakes his gaze over me like he's debating on whether to fuck me properly or walk away. In the end, he chooses the latter.

When the restroom door closes, I unlock my knees and let them buckle. Crouched down with my head in my hands, I take some deep breaths and try to slow my racing pulse as I debate whether I've lost my sanity completely or only in the presence of one Chance Danvers.

My phone dings. I anxiously dig it out from my pocket to find a new text message that kicks up the butterflies in my belly all over again.

Welcome to my menu, Jane.

Chapter Ten

JANE

"I can't believe you're withholding information out of spite," Addison pouts. "You should be *thanking* me for sending you a Thor look-alike sex god, not punishing me."

"Careful, Addie. You'll get frown wrinkles." I glance over at where she's running on the treadmill next to me and chuckle as her scowl deepens at the thought. It's not like a few wrinkles would mar her natural good looks. Even dotted with sweat, blond hair in a ponytail, and no makeup, my best friend is gorgeous. In her powder-blue sports bra and black spandex capris, she looks like she's in a commercial for NordicTrack.

However, the reflection staring back at me in the wall of windows is a bit more of a hot mess. Damp sections of my hair have escaped my elastic and are now plastered to the sides of my face and neck. I'm wearing identical pants in a heather gray, but I prefer to wear loose, non-tummy baring tank tops and mine is already soaked through after only ten minutes of jogging. I won't be getting asked to sell gym equipment anytime soon.

"Come on, Janey, you can't tell me he basically staked out your IHOP until you showed up for work and then leave it at that."

I still couldn't believe Chance had shown up to the restaurant several times just to see me, but Sally doesn't make a habit of lying. I try to hide my smile by wiping my face with the small towel and say, "Sure I can."

"Fine. Then maybe I'll order up a Handyman Special of my own and ask *him* to tell me what's going on."

A flash of jealousy surges to the front of my brain, taking me by surprise before I can shut it down. Whoa. Apparently I get a little territorial at the thought of other women sticking their hands in my cookie jar. Or on my man candy. Good thing this is only a temporary and casual arrangement. Hear that, Brain? Temporary and casual! Still, that doesn't mean I want to share him with Addison.

I turn my head to see a smarmy grin on her face. She's just crazy enough to do it, so I give in. Besides, it's not like I actually planned to keep anything from her. She might be obnoxious at times, but she's still my best friend, and porn addiction aside, we don't keep secrets from each other. However, that doesn't mean she needs to know every dirty little detail, either.

After making sure that no one is within earshot—we're the only two killing ourselves with cardio on our lunch hour, and the gym rats are all weightlifting on the other side of the room behind us—I discreetly tell her the story of how Chance followed me into the restroom, along with a few highpoints.

"Oh my God," she practically shouts. "He gave you an *orgasm in a public bathroom*?"

I whip my head around to shush her, so fast that I lose my footing. A strangled scream escapes me as I go down, the belt shooting me off the back of the treadmill like a human torpedo to land in a heap at the feet of Kyle, the gym's biggest bodybuilder and token male chauvinist.

"Whoa, are you okay? Here, let me help you up," he says, sounding surprisingly sincere. "You know, babe, there are less painful ways to throw yourself at me."

And he's back, ladies and gentlemen. Utter humiliation prevents me from responding—or maybe my brain is scrambled from going Mach 10; I'm not entirely sure—but I let Kyle help me up as Addie rushes over. "Holy shit, Janey, what are you trying to do, give me a heart attack?"

"Yeah, that was my goal," I answer wryly as I finally get on my feet. "I noticed your heart rate wasn't high enough so I thought I'd give you a little extra jolt. You're welcome."

Kyle, apparently satisfied that I'm going to live, looks between Addie and me with a creeper grin, if I've ever seen one. "What's this I hear about orgasms in bathrooms?"

I throw my hands up in the air, but Addison is quick to reply. "Oh, that? We were just listing all the things you'll never have, like normal-sized testicles and the ability to put your arms down at your sides. But you keep juicin', big guy. I'm sure someday you'll find a girl with a thing for guys with huge boobs and unusually small balls. Come on, Janey, let's go."

Gathering me into her side, she leads me away from Kyle, and I can't help but giggle at his confused expression, like he's not quite sure if he's been insulted. I might feel bad for him if he didn't leer at every girl in the gym and spout off sexist remarks between reps and taking selfies of himself flexing in the mirror.

Once in the locker room, Addie and I grab our toiletry bags and head for the showers. Since she hasn't said anything since my Treadmill Torpedo stunt, I'm thinking I might get away without an inquisition, but I should have known better. This is Addison Paige we're talking about, the human bloodhound who sniffs out secrets for business and pleasure.

"So are you going to see him again?" she calls to me as she lathers up her hair. "Please, God, tell me you're going to see him again, Janey."

I bite my lip as images from last night flood my memory. After our little tryst in the bathroom on Monday morning, I jumped every time my phone dinged, but I didn't hear from him until late that night when he texted to let me know that he had planned on coming over but something had changed on him last minute. I told him it was fine and left it at that. It's not like we'd made plans or anything. But then my phone rang, and when I answered it, his gruff command had me wet in seconds.

"Lay down and put the phone on speaker. I want one hand pinching your nipples and the other fucking your hot cunt."

I've never had phone sex before. A previous boyfriend had talked about doing it, but the way he described it made it sound like I'd be playing the role of a phone sex operator to get him off, which held all the appeal of a root canal. I told him I was too shy for that kind of thing, and that was the last we discussed it.

That's not at all what phone sex with Chance had been like. I don't even think he was doing anything on his end of the line—if he was, he kept it to himself. The entire conversation couldn't have lasted more than five minutes. There was no flirting, no slow seduction. Just husky instructions on the lascivious things he wanted me to do, and explicit descriptions of what he'd be doing if he were there with me. He talked me through fucking myself to a stratospheric climax that was ten times better than any masturbation session with a Magic Wand had given me. After I came back to myself, and my breaths evened out, he said, "Sleep well, Jane," and hung up.

But as good as that was, it wasn't as hot as what he did the following night. Or rather, this morning, if we're being technical.

"Well?" Addison prods.

"We kind of struck an agreement."

You would have thought she was a dog and I'd just waved a tennis ball in front of her face. "What kind of agreement?"

Pouring strawberry-scented conditioner into my palm, I feel an impish grin curl the corners of my mouth. "The sex-with-no-strings kind."

"Shut. *Up!* I'm torn between being so happy for you that I'd risk serious injury doing a happy dance in these slick conditions, and wishing I'd called him for myself."

I laugh as I tilt my head back to rinse my hair.

"Have you seen him since the restaurant? Wait, don't tell me, I'm getting super jealous. I don't need to know. Okay, I lied. I totally need to know. Tell me."

Oh, I saw him all right. I didn't think I was going to, since he told me he had a meeting with the P4H guys, but I'd held out hope for a repeat of Monday night's phone call. I finally forced myself to go to bed at ten p.m. because I had to work the early shift at the restaurant this morning and needed to get at least a few hours of sleep. Though I knew it was ridiculous, I was disappointed I hadn't heard from him. But it's not like we're dating, for fuck's sake, so he doesn't have to contact me for any reason, nor should I expect him to.

That's why I was surprised as hell when my phone rang at two a.m., fifteen minutes before my alarm was due to go off.

"Chance?" I'd said, my voice raspy with sleep and concern as I sat halfway up in bed.

"Open your door, Jane."

I'd squinted in the dark at my bedroom door, confused, my brain struggling to wake up and make sense of anything. "It is open."

I hadn't been sure, but it sounded like he might be trying to hide a smile when he spoke next. "Not your bedroom door. Your apartment door."

"Apartment door?"

"Now, Jane."

When I at last opened the door, I found Chance standing on my threshold. He pocketed his phone, stepped inside, and kicked the door shut before pinning me facing the wall. "You should sleep naked from now on. It'll make things easier."

Feeling his hard body pressed against me, and his warm breath fanning over my neck, took me from sleepy to soaked in two-point-six seconds. Much like the phone sex, he didn't waste any time. He shoved our clothes out of the way, buried his cock balls-deep, then started fucking me like a man possessed. It was savage and hurried, with grunts and moans as we chased our releases all the way to the finish line.

We both had our foreheads on the wall, panting like animals, as we tried to find the motivation to move. Moments later, my alarm went off in my bedroom. That did the trick. He put himself back together and said, "Better get in the shower or you'll be late for work." Then he gave me a playful smack on my ass on his way out the door.

It'd been one hell of an awesome start to my day, and I've been smiling almost non-stop ever since.

I turn off the shower and give Addison an evil little smirk as I wring the excess water from my hair. "Since the restaurant, I've enjoyed plenty with him," I say. When she gives me a death stare, I laugh and relent. Sort of. "They rhyme with 'cone hex' and 'sidnight wicky' and if you can't figure them out from that, then tough titty. Serves you right for sending that guy over to my apartment."

"How can you still pretend to be mad about that? I think we've established this is the best thing that's ever happened to us. I mean, you. But, you know, me, indirectly."

"Not Chance," I say, picking up my bag of shower supplies. "The *real* handyman—the one that looked like a walrus— who you sent over Saturday morning. He convinced me to let him check over what Chance did to my sink, and after that he tried sticking around to chat me up. Not cool. For that, you shall be punished."

"Oh, come on, that's not fair. How was I supposed to know the stripper would fix your shit? Janeyyyyyy."

She whines my name as I wrap a towel around myself and stride out of the shower area, leaving her to scramble to turn off the water and get her things together. I do my best to keep my laughter on the inside, but it's not easy because for once I have the upper hand in our friendship. And I'm enjoying the hell out of it. I won't make her suffer for long. Maybe.

When I get to the locker, I check my phone and see a text from Chance. My stomach does a few crazy flips before I can tell it to pipe down.

Chance: *When do u get home from ur day job?*

Me: *6. But I won't be home long. I'm covering the end of someone else's shift tonight at 7.*

Chance: *I'll b there @ 6:15. Be naked.*

"Why are you grinning at your phone like an idiot?" Addie asks as she reaches me. "Oh damn, it's him, isn't it? What'd he say?"

"Nothing too exciting," I quip as I start to dress. "But if I had to guess, I think I'm in for another 'wicky' tonight."

Chapter Eleven

JANE

It's Friday evening and I'm staring at the blinking cursor on my laptop, waiting for the right words to come to me so I can move that fucker across the page and make some progress. But my muse has been on an extended sabbatical and refuses to make an appearance. Again.

This thesis is going to be the death of me. I'm so close to being done, but it's missing an element, and I can't figure out what it is. My dual degree is in social work and women's and gender studies, so I chose to do my thesis on the objectification of women in America—how we're taught we should embrace submission to the desires of men, because the more we do, the more valuable we become.

Believe me, the irony of what I'm writing versus what I'm practicing with my no-strings thing with Chance is not lost on me. I'm a feminist by day, and a woman who enjoys being manhandled and objectified at night. But I'm *choosing* to be treated this way. I wouldn't find it the least bit tolerable if some random guy leered at me like a piece of meat he'd like to stick his dick in.

That's the story I'm telling myself, but as I sit at my dining room table wearing the nicest piece of lingerie I own because a man I've only known for a week told me to, I can't help but feel a little hypocritical.

I pick up my phone and pull up my text messages. There are several from Addie wanting the latest gossip on my newly acquired sex life, but I'm enjoying making her wait for tidbits, so I'll answer those tomorrow. The suspense is still punishment for her little trick a week ago.

Obviously in hindsight, I'm thankful she sent over Chance the Handyman—if she hadn't, I wouldn't be having the best sex of my life with a modern day Viking. But that doesn't mean I'm letting her off easy, and it's driving her crazy. She had her fun last week, now I'm having mine. She gets it; she just doesn't like it.

But it's not one of Addison's texts that I've read over a dozen times since receiving it. It's the one I got from Chance an hour ago.

Just got off. Taking shower & grabbing food. Be there in 1 hr. Wear the sexiest lingerie you own. Nothing else.

Reading his message now elicits the same butterflies-in-the-stomach reaction as it did the first time and every time in between. In fact, *everything* about him causes that reaction. A text, a look, a command, a touch... The long and short of it is, Chance affects me at the cellular level. The man reads me like a book, and there hasn't been a single thing he's said or done that I haven't enjoyed immensely.

Three solid knocks startle me then kick my pulse into high gear. *He's here.* I rush over to the door and pause for a deep breath. Glancing in the mirror that hangs on the wall over my console table, I try fluffing my hair, which I've left down for the first time since we've met, and then I cinch the belt on the short robe that's covering my black lace teddy.

Somehow Chance knows I'm just on the other side of the door, because when he speaks, his voice is commanding, and low enough so that I'm only able to hear him this close. "For every second you make me wait out here, Jane, I'm spanking your sweet ass."

A shiver chases down my spine. That isn't necessarily the threat he intends it to be since I've enjoyed his spankings several times in the last four days. We haven't had much time to see each other, what with both of us working two jobs—him with his construction company and the occasional stripping session, and me with my internship during the day and waitressing after (and sometimes before)—but we managed to sneak in quickies between shifts. Every day he'd come over, screw my brains out, then leave me to get ready as I attempt to scrub away my freshly-fucked look with a two-minute shower before heading to the restaurant.

But Chance wanted to make plans for a night where we aren't rushed, and thankfully I never have to waitress on Fridays. It's the one concession to my schedule since I work a lot of the crappy three to seven a.m. half shifts that no one wants, and by the end of the week, I need Friday off to do absolutely nothing.

"You're already at ten, Jane."

Shit. I throw the lock and open the door. Every time I see him, I'm still in awe that someone as sexy as him wants to be with someone like me. But I'm no dummy; I'm not about to ask him why or question his actions. If he's going to be judgment-impaired, that's on him, and I plan on riding out this little miracle for as long as possible.

"Hi," I say, hating the tiny tremor in my voice. I'm more nervous than usual.

Goddamn, he's gorgeous. His hair is hanging loose and

still wet from his shower. Wait, no, he's wet everywhere. Water drips down his face, from the tips of his spiked eyelashes and the end of his nose. His white T-shirt clings to his shoulders and chest, showing every ridge of his muscles, the dusting of hair, his dusky nipples.

"You're wet."

He raises an eyebrow. "It's raining, and I had to park a block away."

As though he's summoned it to underscore his claim, lightning flashes through my kitchen window, followed by a distant rumble of thunder. I'd been so lost in thought about his arrival I hadn't even heard the storm.

"Well, come in. We can take your clothes to the laundry room down the hall and stick them in the dryer if you want." I ogle his firm ass in the damp jeans as he passes me. I smirk. "You'll have to lounge around in your underwear for a while, but I'm surprisingly okay with that."

"You are, huh?" He sets a plastic bag I hadn't noticed until now on the kitchen counter. "Nice to know you don't hold issue with me in a state of undress around your delicate sensibilities."

"I try not to be too prudish," I quip. "What's in the bag?"

"Chinese." The answer makes me frown in confusion. "Told you I was grabbing food."

"I know, but I thought you meant you were grabbing something to eat before coming over. I didn't expect you to bring me—us—dinner." Because correct me if I'm wrong, but that's kind of a date-ish thing to do. And nothing about this arrangement is date-ish. The whole point of it is to *not* be date-ish.

Chance grabs the hem of his shirt and peels the wet material up and over his head, depositing it into the sink. "You already eat?"

"No, actually, I—"

"Why are you wearing a robe?"

I glance down at my soft, pink robe as if to confirm it's still there, then look back up when I hear the sound of his belt coming undone.

"Please tell me that's not the sexiest lingerie you own."

I swallow thickly. "It's underneath."

"I specifically remember telling you to wear nothing else. Where are your glasses?"

"I felt a little silly sitting around in lingerie while working, and they're over by my laptop. I don't need them to see close up."

"Show me." I go to where I'd been set up in the dining room and grab my glasses. When I turn around, he's right there, crowding me against the table. "Put 'em on. There," he says after I follow his instructions, "I like you with them on. The 'sexy librarian' looks good on you, Jane."

"Social worker."

"What?"

"I'm not a librarian, I'm a social worker. Or at least I will be if I ever finish this damn thesis. That's what I was working on before you came over."

"Interesting." He seems to think about that. I wish I had access to those thoughts. Does he really think it's interesting, or is he simply patronizing me? I don't know him well enough. After several long moments, he peers over at my laptop and then grins back at me. "Sure you weren't watching porn, dirty girl? I know how much you enjoy your kinky videos."

I chuckle. "Are you kidding? I haven't watched porn since—"

Oops. Admitting something like this could be too much. Nothing about our lives is supposed to change due to this arrangement. It's one of the unwritten rules of no-strings sex.

He narrows those clear, blue eyes at me. "Since when?"

I bite the corner of my lower lip. Chance plunges a hand into the back of my hair, grabs a fistful, and yanks it back. "Since when, Jane?"

A shot of adrenaline turns my bloodstream into the Indy 500, and the sharp sting at my scalp triggers warmth to flood my sex.

"Since we started our thing," I say in a breathy tone.

He dips his head and runs his nose up the length of my throat. "You mean since I started fucking you."

"Yes."

"Because I satisfy your needs. Because getting fucked by me is better than watching porn."

They aren't questions, they're statements. True ones. And the arrogant bastard knows it. Still, I appease him and respond, because it's part of the game. "God, yes."

"Good girl. Now take off this fucking robe, and the next time I say 'nothing else' there damn well better be nothing else. Understand?"

I nod and quickly shed the robe, dropping it somewhere off to the side. He releases his hold on my hair and takes a step back to let his gaze roam over me, slow as he pleases. My hands grip the edge of the table behind me as I force myself not to fidget with insecurity. A vixen in the bedroom (or anywhere else), I am not. I might be open and modern-thinking when it comes to my sex life, but I don't know how to harness my sexuality and use it to seduce. That's Addison's department. If you want to psychoanalyze something, I'm definitely your girl. But embracing the sex kitten within? Not so much.

Chance palms my breasts over the demi-cups. He squeezes each mound and pinches my nipples through the lace. My breath catches, and my clit throbs in anticipation in time with my heartbeat. I moan softly and drop my head back as my eyes drift closed, letting my other senses take over as he maps out my body with his strong hands.

"This is a pleasant surprise. It's the perfect balance of wicked and classy. Black lace becomes you, Jane." It's a sheer one-piece, cut high on the sides and low in the back with spaghetti straps. I'm glad he likes it because it's the only thing like it that I own. "Why do you have it?"

My eyes snap open and I meet his gaze. "Excuse me?"

"Either a man bought it for you, or you bought it for a man. Which is it?"

I flash back to the night I came out of the bathroom and surprised Justin after purchasing it that afternoon. It was my attempt to spice up our sex life. He'd taken one look at me and frowned in disappointment, asking how much I spent on something so frivolous. Then he proceeded to tell me that lingerie was pointless since it only served its purpose for a minute at most before it ended up on the floor. We never even had sex that night.

"I bought it for a man."

Chance grunts, and I get the feeling that this answer is only slightly better than if I'd said a man had bought it for me. "And did he lose his mind when he saw you? Get hard so fast he had to undo his pants to relieve the pressure?"

The air in my lungs gets stuck as I watch him undo the fly of his jeans and adjust his hard cock so it's not pinned down by the wet denim. To know that I've affected him with my appearance gives me a small taste of power—something that, by design, I normally don't feel in our sexual encounters— and boosts my confidence by a couple notches.

"No," I say. "He said it was a waste of money and told me to return it."

A storm passes over his face to match the one raging outside my apartment. "Then he was a fucking moron. I promise you it's worth every penny you paid. You look sexy as hell, like a pinup without the heels."

Shit, I didn't think about heels. "You want me to grab a

pair?"

He gives me a crooked grin that makes my knees weak as he lifts me by the hips and plants my ass on the table. Stepping between my legs, he says, "Normally I'd say yes, but I like you better without. I've never met anyone who straddles the fence between devil and angel as well as you, Jane. Other women try to play at one or the other, but you don't have to. You're equally both, and I'm finding it's a combination I can't get enough of."

"Oh."

"Yeah. Oh," he says, then tears my bodice in half, right down the middle.

Chapter Twelve

CHANCE

Jane gasps and looks down at the tattered ruins of her lingerie. "I thought you said you *liked* it!"

"I do. But I don't like that it was bought for another man."

I fucking hate it, actually. Like, acid-churning-in-my-gut hate it. It doesn't matter if the asshole never touched her in it. I want it off her and gone. "I'll open a line of credit somewhere, and you can get as much pointless underwear as you want." She opens her mouth to argue—because I might not know a lot about this woman, but I've gleaned enough to know she's incredibly proud and independent—so I stop her. "Save it, Jane. The only thing I want your mouth doing right now is sucking my fat cock. Turn around and lie on your back with your head hanging off the edge of the table."

She stares at me like she's trying to figure me out. The last thing I need is her attempting to piece together my puzzle. I prefer my parts scattered when it comes to women, and that's how I intend to keep it. Reaching down, I pick up her fluffy pink robe. "Every second you stall adds to the spanking punishment, baby. Keep this up and you won't be able to sit for a week."

That gets her attention, and she scurries to do my bidding. Her obedience is such a fucking turn-on. So are her slight frame and pert tits. I love that she wore her hair down tonight, with waves falling around her shoulders, long and loose so I can wrap it around my hands to control the angle of her head and the arch of her graceful neck. Damn, I have a thing for her neck. Don't ask me why. I'm usually an ass man, but her throat attracts me like I have a sudden case of vampirism.

Then there's her black-rimmed, rectangular glasses that give her the hot librarian—sorry, *social worker*—look that makes me want to fuck the primness right out of her. Except she doesn't have a prim bone in her body. No, my Jane is as dirty as they come, and I fucking love it.

Jesus, I just said *my* Jane. That's not what I mean. I don't mean she's *mine*. I used it to clarify that I'm talking about *this* Jane and not any of the others out there.

Anyone argues anything different and we'll have problems.

As she gets into position, I place the robe on the edge of the table to give her some padding for her neck. I want her head hanging off the side for a very specific reason. I tuck my thumbs into the sides of my jeans and boxer briefs and push them over my hips, letting my hard cock spring free. I hear her quick intake of breath as it bobs above her face.

My height gives me an advantage in this position for the perfect upside-down blow job. All week I've been thinking about doing this with her, but wanted to wait until we aren't rushed. Because that fascination I have with her throat? It's about to get a whole lot better.

Stroking myself, I step in close. "Why don't you get me warmed up and show my balls some love."

I bite back my groan as her tongue snakes out to lick over my stones then suck them into her mouth one at a time. Judging by the sounds she's making, you'd think she's eating a decadent dessert she can't get enough of. It's one of the many things I find so fucking hot about Jane Wendall. Women who pose and try to look sexy while blowing aren't doing it because *they* enjoy it. They're doing what they think I want and acting how they think *I* want them to act, all fake doe eyes and false coyness. It's annoying, but I ignore it and enjoy the blowjob all the same.

But Jane is different. She's not fake. She's not doing it solely to get something in return, because those things are just as much for her as they are for me. Every look she gives me, every touch, every sound she makes, proves that she genuinely loves servicing me. It's the biggest fucking turn-on, and for the first time in my life, I want to make her scream for other reasons than ego.

Ego's part of it, but with her it's more than that. I want to make her feel good. I want her to get every bit as much pleasure out of this as I do. Watching her break apart under me as her insides convulse around me is the greatest high, and it's addicting as hell.

"Good girl," I rasp and take a step back to give her a breather. "Did sucking my balls make you wet?" She nods. "Use your hands and show me. Get them coated with that sweet honey from your pussy."

I continue to stroke myself as I watch her hands dip between her legs. She holds them up for me to see, shiny with slickness. "Now rub it all over my cock so you can taste both of us when I fuck your mouth." I surrender my shaft to her delicate hands as she works to cover me, twisting and pulling, driving me damn near to the brink. "Enough," I growl, failing to keep my composure. "Open that pretty mouth of yours, baby."

"Yes," she whispers before opening wide like she was told.

As I slide my dick in her mouth, we both moan. I start with short strokes to get her used to this slightly awkward position, but I don't have to worry. Jane takes me like a pro, keeping her teeth out of the equation and swirling her tongue around the head between my thrusts. "That's real good, Jane, real good. But you can do better, can't you?" She hums an *mm-hmm* and tilts her head back even farther. "Show me. Show me how a slut takes my cock."

I push in again, but this time I don't stop with only a few inches. I keep going until she's swallowed every thick inch, watching with satisfaction when I see myself filling her throat as the front of her neck bulges from my cock. "Yes," I rasp, then pull out all the way to allow her a quick reprieve. She takes a few lungfuls of air before I dive back in, setting up a steady rhythm of thrusting, holding, and retreating.

Her hands go to her tits, and she starts pinching and tugging on her nipples. Fucking hot. I reach down to feel her pussy and find her soaking. It's calling me, begging me to come and play with it, and it's a siren call I can't ignore.

Once again, I pull all the way out. Strings of saliva and pre-cum stretch from her mouth to my dick, and the image makes my balls draw up tight. I don't think a woman has ever looked sexier. "I'm done fucking your mouth, but if you want me to play with your other holes, you'd better not waste any of that pre-cum I'm giving you. Eat up, slut."

She pulls the viscous strands off my cock and moans as she licks and sucks them from her fingers. When she's finished, I help her sit up.

"Whoa," she says, grabbing the sides of her head.

"Bit of a head rush, baby?" I hold her to me, her back to my front, and nip the side of her neck.

She inhales sharply and angles her head to give me better access. Raising her arm, she plunges her fingers into my wet hair, holding me in place. "Everything you to do me gives me a head rush, Chance."

"Oh yeah?" I squeeze her tits and pinch her nipples, making her gasp and arch her back, but I don't let her get far. "You like being my little slut?" She nods. "Tell me why." She continues to writhe from my ministrations, but doesn't answer. I get the feeling she's not only lost in the sensations, but she's also avoiding answering me.

That shit doesn't fly. I'm pretty sure I know why she likes it, but I'm not about to let her disobey a direct order, and I want her to say it out loud.

I slide my hands between her bent legs to her bare sex. I let her believe she's getting away with her elusive behavior and start rubbing the juices from her pussy all over, making sure she's nice and slick. Jane moans and rocks her hips into my hand. I hold one leg down to the table as a preemptive measure, then I slap her pussy. She cries out and instinctively tries to close her legs, but I've made it impossible. She's bare and vulnerable to my punishments.

"I said you'd get spanked, but I never said *where*." A soft mewling sound escapes her. I nip the shell of her ear and give her the order again. "Tell me why you like being my slut, Jane. And don't even think about lying to me or your pussy will be sore for all the wrong reasons."

Again, she hesitates, and it makes the animal inside me claw at its cage as I war between needing her to obey and wanting her to rebel. Either way, things are about to get interesting.

Chapter Thirteen

I briefly consider telling Chance that the light slaps on my bare sex aren't much more of a punishment than the spanks he administers to my ass, but decide against it. Sure, it stings a little initially—especially when I don't know it's coming—but then the heat pools in my core and makes me wetter than I already am.

He wants to know why I like him treating me like his own personal slut. It's not anything profound or psychologically disturbing. In fact, it's probably the most common reason a woman enjoys rough sex mixed with humiliation. But I think it's not the reason that matters to him as much as that I *admit* the reason to him. In doing that, I'm taking ownership of my particular brand of kink instead of merely letting it languish in the shadows of my mind and internet browser.

"Jane?" he asks as he raises his hand, ready to strike me again.

I capture it between mine. "Okay, I'll tell you."

Taking a deep breath, I try to ignore how the head of his cock is prodding my lower back. Even if Chance weren't attached to it, I think I'd have a love affair with his cock—it was that beautiful and felt that amazing.

"I'm listening."

"I've always been *good*. The good daughter, the good student, the good citizen. I like the idea of being *bad* without any real life repercussions. I like how with you I can be dirty and bad and just plain wrong, and it's okay. Though, I'm not sure why the humiliation aspect turns me on so much."

"No reason to analyze it," he says. "Only thing that matters is that it gets you off. Speaking of which…" I sigh as he begins circling my clit with the tip of his finger. "You like that?"

"Mm-hmmm." I arch my back so I have room to grab his cock and stroke it while he pleasures me. The man has magical fingers, magical lips and tongue, a magical cock… yeah, I've decided he's pretty much a unicorn with attitude, aka The Perfect Lover.

"As nice as that feels, I want at that ass," he says, giving me a light tap on my hip. "On your knees, sweetness."

I'm surprised that he called me sweetness. He's used the casual endearment—at least, I *assume* it's meant casually—plenty of times, but never during sex, and I wonder if he's conscious of the slip or if it's escaped him entirely.

I get into position, ass in the air and chest on the table. My breath shudders past my lips. There's no hiding like this. Everything I own is on display. The insecurity and vulnerability floods me, heating me from the inside.

I can't see what he's doing, so I jump a little when his rough hands grab my ass. He chuckles, and I know he loves it when I'm on edge like this. He kneads my cheeks like mounds of dough, spreading them out and back together…out and back together…

I hear the loud *smack* a full second before I feel it. The flesh on my right cheek stings, but I don't shy away from it. Instead, I mewl like a wanton kitten and push my ass up higher. I want more, and he's happy to oblige. His hands rain down slaps one after another to my backside, with intermittent pauses to grab and spread my cheeks so he can see the proof of my arousal.

"Look at you," he says, and I wish I could. I wish I could see what he's doing to me—the raised red welts from his hands, my pussy lips swollen and covered in the juices I can feel dripping down my inner thighs…

"So fucking sloppy wet for me, aren't you?" His fingers stroke my puffy folds, and though he hasn't touched it directly, my clit is so sensitive right now that even glancing over the labia surrounding it makes my body string tight like a bow.

"Yes, Chance," I answer, my voice a breathy moan. "Only for you."

"Good girl. Now hold still, Jane. I'm gonna get this tight pussy even tighter for me. I like making the fit a challenge."

Challenge is an understatement. When he makes me come before entering me, it doesn't matter how wet I am. With his extra large cock and my climax-swollen vagina, the fit is *tight*. And that's not hipster slang for "awesome." Though that works, too.

Spreading my cheeks, he licks through my folds. I cry out as his tongue circles and flicks over my clit. The tension in my belly grows, like a snowball rolling down a hill that gets bigger and bigger—only this ball is made of white-hot fire, and it's burning me up.

I've never been able to orgasm from oral sex until Chance. He's a god at eating pussy. Not some pansy who uses the tip of his tongue to keep his face from getting messy—hell, no. Chance dives in, face and all, and the myriad of sensations he creates—with his tongue, lips, teeth, nose, chin, and even the scruff of his beard—is the most mind-blowing thing I've ever experienced.

"Fuck, you taste good," he rasps. His talented fingers find my clit, and the slow build of my orgasm is suddenly barreling down on me like a freight train. "That's it, Jane. I want you coming in my mouth, on my tongue, until your very essence is permanently imprinted on my taste buds."

Burying his face in my pussy again, he fucks me with his tongue while he continues to rub the bundle of nerves. My legs begin to shake, and I can't hold back the keening moans tripping from my lips as my climax approaches. Then I squeak, just before all sounds are cut off as everything in me tenses, and the ball of fiery sensations bursts like a match thrown into a pile of fireworks.

Chance digs his fingers into the soft flesh of my upper thighs, making animalistic noises as he greedily drinks everything my body offers him, and I tremble with the aftershocks. Finally, he pulls away, and I turn my face to look over my shoulder as he straightens and swipes a hand over his mouth and chin, cleaning off the juices I left behind.

Eyes dark with passion hold my gaze as he pushes a single, thick finger inside my swollen channel, testing my readiness for him. I can feel how tightly I'm gripping his finger, and I'm not sure if I'm ready at all. That was one of the most powerful orgasms I've ever had.

"You'll never fit. Not like this."

With his free hand, he smacks the tender globe of my ass.

"Oh my fucking God," I say weakly, shocked I already have a second climax stirring.

"That's for doubting me. And now I prove you wrong."

He removes the rest of his clothes then helps me off the table to stand in front of him. "Bend over the table and bring your right leg so you're open to me."

I do, pressing my breasts against the warm wood then bending my right knee and tucking my leg up along my side.

A second later I feel his dick swipe through my wet pussy lips several times before he lines himself up...and proves me wrong.

It takes probably an entire minute, but with teasing my clit and using short strokes that lengthen every time, he's fully seated. Our breaths are erratic, our bodies covered in sweat— proof that the last sixty seconds had been the best kind of torture on both of us, and now we get our reward. Good. Hard. Fucking.

Except he's not moving, and it's driving me insane. I mewl in frustration and arch my hips to spur him into action, but it only earns me another spanking, one that makes me yelp and my pussy ache even more. Yanking my head back by my hair, he leans over me and speaks into my ear. "I'll fuck you when I'm good and goddamn ready. You're not the one in control here. *I am*, aren't I?"

I lick my lips and nod as best I can.

"Say it," he growls.

"You're the one in control," I whisper.

He pinches a nipple. I cry out as the brief flash of pain travels at light speed to my clit and sends a rush of warmth between my legs. "Louder."

"You're in control!"

"And who does your cunt belong to?"

"You," I say reverently, because I want it to be true. "My cunt belongs to you."

"Goddamn right it does. I'm gonna make sure you don't forget it."

He barely finishes his sentence before he starts a furious rhythm, drilling into me like a jackhammer with one hand braced on my lower back and the other still anchored and pulling back on my hair to keep my body bowed taut.

Over and over, he slams into me, and I lose myself in the sensations. His hips smacking against my ass. His cock invading me, its veiny ridges raking gloriously over the nerve-rich flesh of my vagina. The lovely sting at my scalp sending frissons of electricity to every erogenous zone in my body. All of it threatens to consume me, to pull me under the riptide of unbelievable pleasure and drown me.

But just as I'm about to succumb to my second orgasm, Chance pulls out. I whimper in protest, but don't dare move my hips or try to entice him back. This is his game; he's in control. I admitted as much a few minutes ago, so now I have to trust that he won't make either of us suffer for long.

He swipes a thumb through my wetness and runs it up to my puckered hole, causing me to jerk and draw in a sharp breath. Rubbing in slow circles, he teases me with the carnal promise of more. "I'm fucking your ass tonight, Jane. I've been thinking about doing this ever since I since I shoved a finger in here during our little bathroom encounter. I could tell by your reaction you either don't have a lot of experience with anal, or none at all. Which is it?"

"N-none," I stammer.

Chance gives a pleased grunt and pushes, slow and steady, until his thumb passes the ring of muscle trying to keep it out. I moan softly as he moves it in and out, stretching the sides and opening me up. The sensitive nerve endings come alive and send ripples of pleasure up my spine.

He switches his thumb out for two fingers. I know enough by now to concentrate on relaxing my muscles, and that when I feel the need to tighten them, I actually need to push out in order to let him in. But that doesn't mean I'm all that good at it.

I suck in a sharp breath as he tries to add a third finger, and I instinctively bear down. He stops for a second and dips a digit from his other hand into my still soaking pussy, rubbing the tip along the ridges of my G-spot and reminding my body that it wants whatever he does, no matter *what* he does.

"Atta girl, Jane," he says. "You know how big my fucking cock is. I'm trying to do you a favor and prepare you first, because make no mistake, my cock is going in your tight little asshole either way."

In the back of my mind, I know Chance won't do anything that would make something hurt in a bad way. Any pain he gives me is the good kind. But pretending he doesn't care, as if the only pleasure that truly matters is his own, makes my pulse race as flames of desire lick over my skin.

"We'll try one more time and then ready or not, here I come. No pun intended." He chuckles without mirth, like a mad scientist about to throw the switch on his creation. "Spread your ass for me."

I reach back, grab my cheeks, and pull them apart. All of my weight is on my chest and face, but I'm angled so that I can see him. Watching him watch me, seeing his different expressions as he fucks me… Goddamn, it's so hot.

He removes the finger from my pussy, and I whimper before I can stop myself. Flicking his gaze to mine, he gives me an evil grin, then leans forward and spits on my asshole. I gasp as I feel it hit my sensitive ring and start to slide down my crack. But my shock is replaced with ecstasy when he scoops up the saliva with his thumb and works it around my rim, allowing that third finger to finally slide into my hole. I moan and press my hips back, begging him for more, which he gives me.

I don't know if it's a minute or five or twenty that he works me open, fucking me with his fingers as he stretches me wider and wider until he's satisfied his dick will have few issues getting past my body's natural instinct to keep that area "exit only." Sweat slicks my skin, and my breathing is erratic at best, but I'm anxious for him to take my last claim to virginity.

"Please, Chance, fuck me," I beg. "Fuck my ass."

Finally, he presses the bulbous head of his cock against my

back hole. Though he'd opened me up a lot with his fingers, as soon as he retreated, things immediately started tightening up. I feel the pressure of being stretched all over again, but it's not nearly as bad as in the beginning. I remind myself to take deep breaths and push back as he steadily pushes forward, but it's starting to sting. Jesus Christ, he's big.

Just as I'm thinking I can't do this, he withdraws.

I hear something else tear open, and I lift my head up to look over my shoulder. It's a small, flat package of—*shit, that's cold*—lube, I realize as he rubs it in. I look at him questioningly and he answers with a crooked grin—not the kind his evil alter ego gives me when we're playing, but the genuine smirk he gives me all the time—and I get what he's done. He let me ride the edge of the unknown with the twinges of apprehension until the last possible second, and now he's making sure I'm okay—that he doesn't do anything that will cause me true discomfort—and my heart beats a little faster for reasons I don't want to acknowledge.

Donning his stern expression again, he commands me to resume my position, which I do. This time, there's still the pressure, but the lube helps him slide in much easier.

"Ohhhhh," I say on an exhale. "That's…you're…oh my God."

I can't string a full sentence together to save my life as he fully seats himself inside me, and the moan he lets out is sexy as hell. Withdrawing, he hisses in a breath then blows it out as he presses back in. A couple more slow strokes, allowing me to adjust to his size and the new invasion, and then he starts to pick up speed.

The pleasure is different but powerful, and I feel the stirrings of a climax forming in the pit of my stomach. In the distance, as though I'm having an out of body experience, I hear myself making all kinds of sounds—moans, whimpers, mewls, and occasional repetitions of the words "yes" and "more"—but what I focus on are the noises Chance makes. His grunts punctuate every thrust, and his heavy panting tells me he's just as affected as I am.

"Fuck, yes," he grinds out through clenched teeth. "Squeeze my cock just like that, baby."

"Feels so good."

"Goddamn right it does." He slips his hand between me and the table. "And it's about to get a lot fucking better."

Chapter Fourteen

This woman is blowing my fucking mind. I need her to come like yesterday because I'm about to blow a whole lot more, and there's no way I'm not making sure she gets hers first.

I shove my hand under her body and plunge three fingers deep into her pussy. Her back bows, and she cries a string of filthy obscenities that turn me on even more, if that's possible. I love it when my good girl goes bad.

Between how tight she is from coming earlier, and my cock stretching her ass, Jane is filled to capacity, but I don't have any problems pushing my way in because her cunt is soaking wet. She's literally dripping off my knuckles, onto the table, and down her thigh. Everything's a sloppy mess, and I fucking love it.

I press the heel of my hand against her clit as I pump into her with my fingers and cock. She starts chanting, "Oh my God, oh my God, oh my God," and I can tell her orgasm is closing in fast by the way she furrows her brow and she bites down so hard on her lower lip she might draw blood.

"Now, baby," I demand. "Come on me right fucking now."

Screaming, she does, and her pussy squeezes so hard that it forces my fingers from her body so I switch to palming her hips to pull her into me as I continue to thrust, pounding into her, relentlessly chasing my own end.

Lightning shoots through me and starts a fire in my heavy balls. Just as I'm about to come, I pull out. I have a sudden, inexplicable need to see myself fill this woman with my seed, marking her in the most intimate way I can. She starts to push up to see what I'm doing, but I press a hand to the base of her spine to keep her from moving my target.

"Don't move." I fist my cock and jerk myself the last few times before I find my release. I watch with satisfaction as my cum shoots out from the tip of my dick. Most of it lands on her still gaping asshole—which is a thing of fucking beauty in and of itself—but some of it drips down her crack on its way to her pussy.

Shuddering as the last aftershock rolls through me, leaving me with nothing left to spend, I abandon my softening cock and use my fingers to push every drop of cum I spilled on her into her still slightly open hole.

"What are you doing?" she asks meekly.

My gaze flicks up to hers. Her cheeks are flushed, and her face is tucked behind her shoulder. My good girl is back and feeling shy, which is enough to make my dick twitch despite how spent it is. "I want my cum filling you, branding you from the inside." When I have the outside of her completely cleaned up, I tap the pad of my thumb on her puckering rim. "Close it up tight, baby." And she does.

I help her off the table, holding her steady until I'm sure her legs will hold her. I give her a hug, a kiss on the temple, and a light pat on the butt. "Go grab a shower. I'll clean up out here and get dinner set up."

"Okay," she says, with a sweet, sated smile that makes me feel like a man who's done his woman proud.

Then she grabs her robe, holds it to her chest in pointless modestly, and I watch her pad down the hallway to her bathroom. She gives me one last look over her shoulder with those fathomless brown eyes, then disappears and closes the door behind her.

I let out the breath I'd been holding, feeling like I just got kicked in the nuts. The kick actually feels a lot higher than that, but I tell myself that it's only a side effect of having the best sex of my life. Because lying to yourself is fucking fun as hell.

Fifteen minutes later, I hear Jane reenter the apartment after taking my jeans and shirt down to the laundry as I'm setting out the different takeout containers in the living room. I already cleaned her dining table while she took her shower. It was the least I could do, considering the mess I made on it with her. I have to stop reliving it, or I'll be sporting wood while we eat and she'll think I have an erotic reaction to General Tso's chicken. I like the stuff, but not *that* fucking much.

No, what I do like that fucking much is Jane. Every time we have sex, it replaces the last front-runner for Hottest Sex I've Ever Had. I don't even know how that's possible, but I try not to analyze it too much because I don't want to start convincing myself that it means things that it doesn't. We're compatible in the bedroom—which is a figure of speech, considering we've never actually had sex in a bedroom. End of story.

So then why'd you bring over dinner and plan to hang out afterward, asshole? It's the question that's been plaguing me ever since I ordered for two. But just because I don't plan on pulling a hit-it-and-quit-it tonight, doesn't mean I'm looking for anything more than what we have. It also doesn't mean that I can't share a meal and hang out with someone other than the guys on occasion. If that someone happens to be the woman I'm fucking, it's all the more convenient for me.

Jane pads barefoot into the living room in that fuzzy pink robe, the waves of her hair slightly damp from the shower, and a shy smile curving her bee-stung lips. Something kicks up in my gut, and a distant voice in the back of my mind reminds me that in another life, another time, I would've held on to a girl like Jane and never let her go. But I've been down that road before. It only leads to disappointment and heartache, and I'm not interested in feeling either of those things where a woman is concerned—never again.

"Hope you don't mind I brought everything in here." I gesture to the containers on the coffee table.

"Not at all," she says, sitting on the couch and tucking her feet under her butt. "I eat in here all the time. It feels awkward sitting at a formal table all by myself."

"I'm the same way. I'll eat in my living room or at the island in my kitchen, unless I have the guys over. Roman's fine, but Austin's notorious for spilling shit. No way am I letting him near my white carpet with any kind of food."

We divvy up the entrees, and I join her on the couch and dig in. With the long hours at work and the mind-blowing sex, I'm hungry as hell.

"Roman and Austin," she says. "Those were the guys with you at the restaurant, right?"

"Yeah, they're like my brothers. We met each other freshman year in high school, in after-school detention. We were involved in different things, so our social paths probably wouldn't have crossed otherwise, but our personalities clicked, and we've been best friends ever since."

"I can only imagine the trouble the three of you caused as teenagers," she says, glancing over at me with a small grin.

"Who, us?" I ask incredulously, pointing at myself with

my chopsticks. "We were angels. They were never able to prove otherwise."

"Mmhmm, I'll just bet. And then the angels grew up to be strippers. How did that happen?"

I smile, remembering the drunken night the guys and I came up with the harebrained scheme that had evolved into a lucrative side business. "It started as kind of a joke in college when we told some girls we'd come to their party and strip for beer and singles. They took us up on it. Word spread, and it wasn't long before we made it a legitimate business."

"Wow, that's actually kind of genius."

I chuckle and run a hand through my mostly dry hair, pushing it away from my face. "I don't know whether to thank you for the compliment or be insulted at how surprised you sound."

"No, I'm not surprised you thought of it," she says quickly in her defense. "I'm more surprised there aren't entire stripper fraternities out there. Seems like it'd be every college guy's dream job."

"I don't know about dream job, but it's not exactly torture getting attention from beautiful women like yourself."

A hint of color spreads over the apples of her cheeks, and she clears her throat. I wonder if she's uncomfortable because I called her beautiful or mentioned dancing for other women. I don't like the idea of it being the latter and resolve to be more careful in the future. Just because she's cool with what I do when I'm not with her doesn't mean I have to be an asshole and rub it in her face.

"Thanks for taking my stuff down to the dryer."

"It's no problem. I'm sorry I don't have anything here to offer you in the meantime," she says between bites, while staring intently at her beef and broccoli. "I feel bad that you're sitting around practically naked."

It was lucky I happened to wear boxer briefs today, or

I'd be a lot more naked. Not that I'd give a fuck, but Jane would probably blush to death, or hurt herself trying not to look at my junk. I've noticed she's only been giving me cursory glances, like she's afraid if she allows anything more, her eyes will wander below my neck. "Doesn't bother me any. I'm practically a nudist at home, and it's not like you haven't seen it all, anyway."

"That's true."

"Jane, you don't have to avert your eyes," I say, smiling big. I can't help it; the woman amuses me to no end. "I'm a stripper, remember? Being stared at for my pretty packaging is as normal as a handshake to me."

At that, she peeks up at me through her dark eyelashes and chews on her lower lip for a few seconds while she thinks, then she turns her attention back to the dinner she's currently prodding with chopsticks. "Just because you're used to being objectified doesn't make it right for me to do it, no matter how pretty I think your packaging is."

I chuckle. "That's either the worst pick-up line I've ever heard, or the best."

Finally, she raises her head and meets my gaze head on. She's trying not to smile, but it's not quite working, and I see a hint of a dimple in her left cheek. I'm surprised I haven't noticed it until now. Then again, when I think about it, I'm not sure she's smiled around me before. She's usually pissed off or turned on, neither of which elicits a dimpled kind of smile. A shame, really, because I'm betting it's pretty fucking great.

"It's not a pick-up line, you Neanderthal. It's my thesis."

I shove my mouth full of chicken and vegetables and consider whether to get into the personal details stuff. On one hand, it's better if we keep everything superficial. No chance of this turning into something neither of us wants if we make everything about the sex.

But on the other hand, the woman intrigues me. I probably

have a hundred questions I want to ask her, stretching from the lame "what's your favorite color?" to more interesting topics like "who was your first kiss?"

Jane clears her throat and turns her attention back to her food. The silence is too long, and now I look like an ass. For fuck's sake, I'm being ridiculous. Getting to know her doesn't mean she'll expect a ring on her finger.

"What's your thesis about?" Her eyes meet mine again. This time, there's a combination of eagerness and hesitancy swirling in those brilliant pools of chocolate, and I realize I don't like the hesitant part one bit. She shouldn't feel like she can't talk to me. "You can't tease me by saying your horrible pick-up line is the subject of your thesis and not explain. Come on," I encourage her, "I'm genuinely curious."

"Okay," she says, stabbing her chopsticks into her container and then setting it on the coffee table. "It's titled 'American Objectification of Women' and explores the stigma that a woman's worth is based on her sexuality or her status as a sex symbol. Also, how we're automatically portrayed in sexual roles that could just as easily be for men, and *not* portrayed in roles that could just as easily be for women."

"You'll have to dumb things down for me, sweetness. Not everyone in the room is as smart as you."

"All right. Take your profession, for example."

"Construction?"

"That wasn't the one I meant, but my point will actually work for both of them." Jane leans forward, her elbows resting on the tops of her thighs. She's getting excited discussing the subject, and it's cool to watch her become more animated. Makes me want to ask more questions, even if I don't necessarily understand the answers. "When someone mentions the word 'stripper,' nine times out of ten they're going to picture a woman. Just like if they hear 'construction worker,' they're most likely to picture a man.

"Go to Google Images and type 'stripper' or even 'exotic dancer' into the search field. Ninety-eight percent of the pictures that come up are women. Now, type in 'doctor' or 'lawyer,' and the images are predominantly men, proving that our perception of women in society hasn't changed as much as we'd like to think."

"Those are points well made, Jane," I say honestly. "So, how much longer before you're done with it?"

"Well, let's see, I've been working on it for about two years, and at the rate I've been going lately…" She squints up at the ceiling and moves her lips as she mentally calculates. I take a swig of my Corona—she'd bought a sixer to have on hand after I'd mentioned in passing that it's my favorite beer—and wait for the verdict. Jane finally levels a serious look in my direction. "I figure I'll be done with it sometime in 2035, give or take."

I almost spray instead of swallow, nearly giving her a beer shower in the process. "I'm not sure whether I'm more stunned by the insane time frame, or the fact you made a joke."

"Hey, I make jokes all the time." She sits up straight, throws her shoulders back, and hitches a perfectly arched eyebrow at me. "I'm actually very funny once you get to know me."

I lean back into the couch then lewdly grab my junk and say, "I think I've gotten to know you pretty intimately." I can't help the chuckle that escapes when her cheeks flush pink, and she balls up her napkin and tosses it at my head. "You opened yourself up for that one, sweetness. Okay, so why won't you finish your thesis until you're eighty?"

"Forty-five."

"Whatever."

"Because I'm missing an element to tie it all together, and I can't figure out what it is. I'm stuck."

"Too bad the Playboys 4 Hire are all dudes." I finish off the rest of my beer and set the bottle on the table. "You could have interviewed our employees about what it's like to be objectified for a living."

"That's sweet of you to offer, but I've already interviewed girls from the Admiral, so I've got that base cov—" Jane's eyes open wide and she slaps the back of the couch, almost startling me. "Wait a minute, that's *it*."

"What's it?"

"Chance, are you serious about that? Because I just realized what could tie everything together. I can do an opposite case study with men who are objectified every bit as much as women, even though society doesn't automatically view them as such."

Damn, she looks fucking cute when she gets excited about her psych shit. I'd be a total asshole to not help her out. The trick would be getting our guys on board.

Playboys 4 Hire is made up of men who are either college students, or have daytime careers. They do it for the money, the pussy, or the rush of dancing and being treated like sex toys, but no matter what their reason, they all had one thing in common: none of them want others to know they're doing it, so we do what we can to make sure their secret is safe.

"As long as you can promise anonymity to those who want it, I don't see why it'd be a problem." The guys might be reluctant, but I'm sure I can talk them into it.

Jane lights up, and she lets out a little squeal as she hops into my lap, straddling me. "Oh my God, Chance, thank you so much!"

Grabbing my face, she kisses me smack on the lips then pulls away, giving me the most radiant smile I've ever seen, and yep, there it is—a dimple drilled into her cheek. I was right; her full smile is pretty fucking great, and it definitely tips the scale toward her innocent side.

Too bad the way her pussy is molding to my cock through the sheer purple panties she'd put on is making me want to tip that scale in the other direction. I slip my hands under her robe, palm her ass cheeks, and squeeze. "I'm afraid there's a price to pay for my help, though."

Instantly, her pupils swallow the brown of her eyes, and her breathing grows shallow. I fucking love the effect I have on her. I don't even have to touch her. My words and tone alone get her wet. She's perfect.

Slipping into her role, she responds, her voice smoky with the carnal lust that already has her dripping cunt making a damp spot on my underwear. "I really want to finish my thesis. Please, I'll do anything you ask."

I raise a dubious brow. "Anything?"

"Yes, sir," she says, lifting up to stroke my hardening cock with her slender fingers. "Anything."

"I think we might be able to work something out."

Unable to stall any longer, I pull her in by the back of her neck and take her mouth as surely as I plan on taking the rest of her at least once more before the night is over.

Chapter Fifteen

JANE

I've never seen so many hot guys in one place at one time. Not even when I went to the strip club years ago did I find so many of the entertainers attractive. But the men of Playboys 4 Hire all rate high on the stunning scale. If there was ever a time I felt out of my depth, it's right here, right now, in this room.

The meeting is being held on a Tuesday night—not many requests for strip shows on a Tuesday—at Chance's place. His gorgeous, completely remodeled, two-story home in Lake Forest. I don't know what I expected his living quarters to be, but a house in the suburbs was *not* it. We're all in the basement, which is set up like a man cave with a bar, pool table, electronic darts, and theater seating in front of a wall holding three flat-screen TVs. The one in the middle is huge, with the ones flanking it about half its size.

Currently, the big one is showing a PowerPoint cued up from Roman's laptop. Never in a million years would I have pictured a room full of male strippers gathered around a PowerPoint presentation, but the three owners of Playboys 4 Hire—Chance plus Roman and Austin, the friends who were with him in IHOP—conduct the meeting every bit as professionally as the board meeting of a large corporation.

Roman had spoken first with a few slides under the heading "Legal and Financial," and Austin's area of expertise had been "New Business and New Recruits." Who knew a company where men took their clothes off for money would have so many mundane things to attend to?

As I'm musing about this, Austin lets out a battle cry from his place in front of the group and crushes a beer can on his forehead, making the entire room go wild.

Okay, so maybe it's not *exactly* like a board meeting. I cover my mouth as I laugh at the antics from where I'm sitting off to the side by the dartboard.

Something soft and furry rubs against my hand, and I look down to see a gray tiger cat, completely unaffected by the chaos and looking for love from the only calm person in the joint. Chance introduced me to Romeo when I'd arrived earlier. No, I'm not making this shit up. The tough-guy bachelor has a *cat* and named him after the famous hero of a romantic tragedy. Contradictory much? *Chance, thy name is dichotomy.*

Mr. Dichotomy holds his hands up and talks loud enough to be heard over the din of the room. "All right, assholes, settle down so we can get to the last topic of the evening." Roman pushes a button on his Mac and a new slide appears on the TV. "Business retention and customer satisfaction."

As the words "customer satisfaction" flash on the screen, the P4H employees whistle, cheer, high-five their buddies, and some even start gyrating their hips, demonstrating how they personally satisfy the customers. Eventually Chance gets them under control and moves through the rest of the slides fairly quickly before Roman takes over to announce upcoming events and work out who'll be doing what.

Watching Chance take command of the room reminds me of all the times he's taken command of me, and I have to cross my legs to relieve some of the ache between my thighs. As though he's mentally tuned into my sex drive's frequency, Chance swings his gaze to meet mine, his eyes a molten navy blue, and the way he's looking at me makes me swear I forgot to get dressed today.

My breath hitches, and his cocky smirk confirms that I'm blushing. I think he keeps track of how many times a day he can make my cheeks flush. He's even taken to texting me vile (fricking hot), detailed descriptions of what he wants to do to me, then he demands that I send him selfies so he can see the effect his words have on me. The man is a complete nuisance.

And I've never been happier—a fact I try not to look too hard at, because if I do, I'll start thinking relationship-y thoughts, and that can't happen. There is no universe in which a guy like Chance wants the responsibility of an actual relationship. So, this is me, not wanting a relationship with a guy like Chance.

A guy who makes me laugh, who asks me how my day was (post-hot-sex, because priorities) and makes sure I eat because half the time I forget or don't have time to fix myself something. A guy who brings me a bag of soothing lozenges when I mentioned my throat is hurting.

Granted, he waves off his consideration by claiming he can't have one of his favorite places to stick his dick out of commission, but that brings me back to the part about making me laugh. Call me immature, but I like his crass humor.

Yeah, okay. I *would* like to date a guy like him. But that's not where this thing is headed, so I'm determined to enjoy what we have while we have it. Full stop.

"Then, if there aren't any more questions," Roman says,

"feel free to finish your beer and pizza and then get the hell out of Chance's house."

"Hold up. One last thing." Chance steps forward and everyone groans as they take their spots again. "Don't get your panties in a twist; this'll only take a second. I'm sure you've all noticed the lovely Ms. Wendall, who sat in on our meeting tonight. She's working on her thesis about what it's like to be viewed as sex symbols and be objectified—"

"It's fucking awesome," says a handsome ginger, to a chorus of laughter and agreement.

Chance crosses his arms and arches a brow in the ginger's direction. "Glad you think so, O'Donnell. You can be Jane's first interview of the night, then."

The humor falls from the jokester's face. "I can't be interviewed about this shit, man. My old man would stop paying for college if he ever found out what I do."

The room fills with murmurs of similar concerns, accompanied by the shaking of heads. I stand and clutch my notebook to my chest. "I know that the appeal of working at Playboys 4 Hire is how careful they are about keeping your true identities under wraps. I'm not looking to out you in any way. The paper will be accessible online, but you can choose to be listed as an anonymous case study."

O'Donnell tilts his head as though thinking about it, then says, "But if you're using us as case studies, aren't you going to want to know about our backgrounds, and what we do when we're not doing this job, things like that?"

I nod. "Yes, that will be part of it."

A swarthy Latino sitting in one of the leather theater chairs chuffs. "Those kinds of details can be just as damning as giving you our names."

More assent and head shaking from the group. It seems this won't work in my favor after all. Looking over at Chance, I give him a shrug and half smile to tell him it's okay and thanks for trying. I watch as his eyes narrow and determination sets in his hard jaw. I know that look. It's the one he gets when I playfully push back against a command. The one that says he's taking offense and accepting a challenge.

Crossing his arms, he scans the crowd and raises his voice. "I'll give a five-hundred-dollar bonus to anyone who participates."

The room is silent for three whole seconds as they stare at Chance in surprise. Then they explode like someone just told them their favorite football team won the Super Bowl, and suddenly I have a line of strippers wanting to answer my questions.

My smile is so big that my cheeks hurt, and something in my chest gets tight. I peer around the gathering men and find Chance. He grins and gives me a wink then turns to talk with Roman and Austin. Oh, shit. I think that tightness in my chest might be my heart swelling. Not good. I need to lock that down right now, before my romantic girly side starts taking over.

Back to business, Janey. Focus on your work.

Sitting down, I lift Romeo from where he's lounging on the chair next to me and gesture for O'Donnell—the first one in line—to have a seat. I hold my hand out. "Thank you so much for doing this."

He accepts my hand, but turns it over and kisses the back of it. "I'm Liam, and spending time with you will be my pleasure."

Another smooth operator, this one, but then I suppose it's a common trait among people whose job it is to seduce. If I'd met sexy Liam a month ago and he'd done the same thing, I would have swooned like a proper female. But since he's not a Thor lookalike who makes me wet every time he pins me with his deep blue eyes…nada.

"Great," I say, taking my hand back. "Then, let's get started."

Chapter Sixteen

"It's a damn good thing looks don't kill, or we'd be looking for a whole new fleet of dancers."

I tear my gaze away from where Jane is interviewing Derrick, one of our newest recruits at P4H, and acknowledge my friend. "You got a point you're trying to make, Reeves?"

Roman takes a pull from his beer, not intimidated in the least by my glare and threatening tone. But he and Austin know they can poke the bear without fear of the bear rearing up and taking a swipe. Anyone else would find themselves with a few new gaps in their smile, but these guys have immunity when it comes to my wrath.

"His point, brother," Austin says with a shit-eating grin, "is that you've shot daggers at every guy who's talked with our Janey there."

"First of all, asshole, there's no 'our' when it comes to Jane," I grind out, making sure I keep my voice low enough so no one else hears me. "And second, if I'm giving anyone dirty looks, it's because she's here in a professional capacity, and every single one of them is flirting with her like she's a goddamn client."

Roman chuckles. "Give the guys a break, man. It's in their nature to charm the panties off a woman, and last I checked, Jane has tits. Hell, *I* wouldn't mind charming my way into her panties. Feel like sharing?"

Do not kill your best friend. Do not *kill your best friend.*

Balling my fists at my sides, I take a deep breath and let it out slowly as I level my gaze at Roman. "I think I'll keep this one to myself, thanks."

He shrugs with a smirk as Austin adds, "Okay, but if you change your mind, let us know, because I am *definitely* down for some ménage action with that one. Is it just me, or do those glasses actually make her look hotter?"

That's it. They're dead.

As I'm contemplating all the ways to hide their bodies, the guys start laughing. "Damn, bro, you've got it bad," Roman says. "Why don't you just admit that you like the girl? Stake your claim already, for fuck's sake."

"Yeah, man, lock that shit down before someone else does." This from Austin. "A girl like that doesn't come around every day."

Don't I fucking know it.

I look over at Jane just as she glances in my direction. She smiles at me, and it feels like the clouds have parted, allowing the warmth of the sun's rays to bathe my face. I give her a wink and revel in the blush that steals across her cheeks. Every time I see it, I get a high I've never gotten from anything else. Not dancing, not stripping, not winning a huge bid... Not even sex. Except for sex with Jane. Because nothing feels better than that.

She clears her throat, tucks her chestnut hair behind one ear, and turns her attention back to Derrick and her notes.

And just like that, the clouds converge and steal my sunshine.

Fuck. The woman has me waxing poetic, and it's been years since that side of me has seen the light of day. You wouldn't guess it knowing me now, but I used to be a pretty big romantic. The guys used to give me shit for it, and called me Romeo, which is where my stripper alias—and my cat's name—comes from. I wasn't all that crazy with the hearts and flowers shit. Really, I was just a thoughtful guy. But when you're a decent guy in a sea of assholes, you come out smelling like a rose and branded "the best guy a girl could ask for." Those were my ex-fiancée's words, not mine.

But that only lasts so long before the subtle manipulation starts, the attempts to mold you into their definition of the perfect man. That's when you either play along and sell your soul to the devil, or throw up your deuces and get the hell out of Dodge.

I'd chosen the latter and made a plan to never again put myself in a position where a woman thinks she has the right to ask me to change who or what I am, or what I do. The plan had been working out great…until I met Jane Wendall.

The woman has "win" written all over her. Sexually, we couldn't be more compatible. I've never seen anyone more beautiful than Jane when she submits to me. It's the biggest fucking turn-on to watch her slip into that headspace.

But beyond the bedroom, she has a quirky sense of humor that constantly takes me by surprise. Whether she's wearing her IHOP uniform, her professional day-job clothes, or pajamas with pandas, I find her breathtakingly beautiful. And since we've started talking a lot more about things other than sex, I've realized how smart she is, and damn if I don't find her brain just as sexy as her body.

She has the old, romantic me asking all kinds of crazy "what if" questions I'm not prepared to answer. And the douchebags I call my best friends are only encouraging him.

"Jane and I have a good thing going with our no-strings arrangement. I don't see any reason to fix what isn't broken."

Roman scoffed. "I'll give you a reason. Jane's not the kind of girl you can treat like a casual fuck forever. It might not be today, and it might not be tomorrow, but eventually she's going to want more. And if she doesn't get it from you, there'll be plenty of guys lined up who are more than willing to give it to her. I can name at least five in this room alone."

The tiny hairs on the back of my neck stand up, and I scan the basement, scouring for signs of who Roman is referring to—the ones who would take Jane from me given the chance.

Fuck that. She's mine, goddamn it, and they can keep their filthy paws to themselves or suffer dismemberment.

"I gotta go," I say, my eyes landing on Jane. "You guys know the way out. See that you find it."

Stalking across the room, I reach where she's sitting and interrupt Derrick. "Sorry, D, but this interview is over for now. If Jane needs anything else from you, I'll let you know." Without waiting for a response from either of them, I grab her hand and pull her to her feet before leading her up to the kitchen on the main floor.

"I'm sorry," she says, "I took too long. It's late, and we're in your house, and—"

"I don't care about any of that." *I can't take another second of watching someone else touching and flirting with what's mine.*

She's looking up at me, waiting for an explanation of my actions—one I'm still trying to wrap my own head around—when she brings her hand up to cover a big yawn. I glance at the clock on the stove. Ten p.m. She's worked two jobs today and then sat in on our meeting and interviewed a dozen people. It's a wonder she's even standing.

"You're beat. Why don't you stay here tonight?"

Jane stares at me in surprise. We haven't spent the night

together before. Not really. Last week when I'd brought over Chinese, we'd fallen asleep on her couch while watching TV. When I woke up at five the next morning with a blanket draped over my body, I found my dry clothes folded on the coffee table in front of me and Jane still snuggled on the other side of the couch in her robe.

She'd woken up at some point, gotten my clothes for me, covered me up, and went back to sleep. After getting dressed, I tucked the blanket around her and watched as she brought it up to her nose and inhaled deeply. A contented smile spread over her face as she tucked the corner beneath her head and continued to sleep. I'd liked that she'd sought out my scent, and I left her apartment that morning a satisfied man for more reasons than just sexual satiation.

"Are you sure?" she asks, her teeth toying with the corner of her lip. "I am pretty beat, but I can totally drive home if it's an imposition."

I give her a small grin. "If it was an imposition, I wouldn't have asked."

"Right, okay, I'm sorry." She chuckles nervously, and I wonder if it's the idea of spending the night at my house, or spending it with me that's making her apprehensive. "Then if you'll point me in the direction of the couch, I'll promptly pass out and leave you to whatever it is you do."

"Yeah, that's not happening. Come on." I grab her hand again and lead her through the house. Romeo bounds up the stairs ahead of us, tail held high in excitement that it's finally bedtime. *Not quite yet, buddy.* I pull Jane into my master bedroom and shut the door behind us so we won't hear the commotion of the guys when they finally leave.

I take the messenger bag from her shoulder and set it off to the side, along with her notebook. "Get undressed," I tell her, "then join me in the bathroom." I'd rather undress her myself, but if I do, I know I won't be able to stop myself from taking her up against the wall, and that's not why I brought her up here.

I've never had a woman in my house before, since I bought it after my ex, Sandra, and I split up. This is my sanctuary, and I've never had the desire to taint it with a parade of random ass. But Jane's different. Despite the fact we started out as fuck buddies, things have somehow shifted. Late at night, when I'm lying in bed and thinking about her, I tell myself that it happened because she's the only one I'm fucking so it's natural to feel some sense of commitment. But even I recognize that for the bullshit that it is.

Jane is different because she's *Jane*. She's unlike anyone I've ever dated—especially Sandra—and I'd have to be dead not to get attached to her.

Running the water in the huge, custom-made, claw-foot tub, I dump in a couple of cups of the powdered mixture of lavender milk that I make myself. It's relaxing and keeps my skin soft and smooth so that I don't have to use lotions. Go ahead and call me a fucking girl, or tell me I have a vagina for taking milk baths, but my day job wreaks havoc on my skin, and I have an aversion to rubbing greasy shit on my body. I have to make sure I'm supremely touchable for the stripping gigs, and I found this alternative regimen that works for me. So, suck it.

"Chance?"

I turn to see Jane standing in the doorway, gloriously naked, with questions in her eyes. I reach out, and she walks over and places her hand in mine. I love that she comes to me without hesitation, so trusting and willing.

"In you go, sweetness." She gingerly steps in, then sinks into the milky water with a contented sigh.

"Oh my God, this is absolutely heavenly," she says, tipping her head back to rest on the curved edge of the tub as she closes her eyes. "Any objections if I set up a permanent residence in your bath?"

I chuckle as I close the door to keep the heat in and Romeo out, then turn the dimmer switch on the overhead light fixture to its lowest setting—just enough to see by without the glaring brightness. "I'll call the post office and have them forward your mail to my master bathroom." She giggles, but even that sounds tired and reminds me that I'm in here to take care of her so I can tuck her into bed.

With me.

I promptly shuck my clothes and lower myself in on the opposite side of the tub, stretching my legs out on either side of her. She'd bent her legs to give me room when I got in, but I want as much of her submerged as possible, so I pull one ankle to rest on my upper thigh and set the heel of her other foot on my stomach. Then, under the water, I use my thumbs to knead her aching foot.

Her eyes fly open as she lets out a gasp that instantly turns into a moan. It's not a sexual one, but my dick is having a hard time telling the difference. *Stand down, asshole. Not tonight.*

"So, I don't mean to sound judgy or anything, but…" She's trying to hide her amusement about something. "A milk bath? Really?"

I grin at her question. "You suck at not sounding judgy, but yes, really. I don't like the way lotions feel, and the lactic acid is great for the skin."

"I knew it." She sits up so fast the water almost sloshes over the side. Pointing a finger at me, she says excitedly, "I knew the first night I met you that you had to have some kind of skin care regimen. You felt way too soft not to. I suppose when you have as many women touching you as you do—"

I don't want to talk right now about all the other women who get to touch me, so I dig one of my thumbs into her arch and her subsequent groan cuts her off, just as I'd intended.

"Holy shit, that feels amazing," she says.

I smirk. "You tell me that all the time, and yet it never gets old."

She rolls her eyes and flicks some water at me, and I chuckle at both my own joke and her reaction. "You would turn that into a sex compliment."

"Of course I would. I'm a crass Neanderthal who only thinks about one thing. I'd hate to ruin my rep by not rising to the occasion. No pun intended."

I set that foot down and start working my magic on the other one. I watch her through the thin veil of steam as she draws her bottom lip between her teeth. The hair around her face is damp and moisture is beading on her skin, making it glow in the low light.

"Then why are you doing all this?" she asks softly.

The mood has shifted from playful to serious, and I have to make the decision to let it ride or shut it down. So naturally, I stall. "What do you mean?"

"Don't play dumb, Chance, you know what I mean. The invitation to stay, the bath, the foot rub. These aren't the actions of a guy who's only thinking about one thing. So, what gives?"

I look down at the milky water where my hands are working on the arch of her foot. I feel as though her eyes are peering straight into my soul right now, and I'm not even sure if *I'm* ready to see what's in there, much less allow her to.

When I don't answer immediately, she continues. "I'm not trying to pressure you into anything. I'm just trying to understand what this is, because it doesn't line up with what you originally said you wanted." I hear her take a deep breath, then she finishes with a hesitant note in her voice. "I don't want to make any assumptions that might ruin things with you. I don't want to lose y—what we have."

I snap my gaze up to hers when I realize what she was going to say. *I don't want to lose you.* I expect it to hit my panic button, to feel that pressure in my chest of being trapped, but it never comes. Instead, I get a little heady knowing that she wants me. And not only in a sexual capacity. She may not have said that in so many words, but I'm not an idiot, and I know how to read between the lines.

Jane wants me. *Me.*

I think.

Fuck, now I'm starting to doubt myself. I can't remember the last time I felt insecure over a girl. Scratch that. I've *never* been insecure over a girl, not even my ex-fiancée. When I realized she didn't want me for who I am, I packed my shit, told her she could pawn the ring, and got the fuck out.

But now I'm finding myself in a predicament where I like a girl—*really* fucking like her—and I'm not sure if she feels the same about me. I know she's into my body and what I do for her sexually, but I'm not a guy known for my deeper substance, so why the fuck would she want more from me?

How 'bout you take your balls out of your purse, put 'em back where they belong, and find the hell out?

My subconscious can be such an asshole sometimes. But it's never wrong.

"C'm'ere," I say, leaning forward and pulling her over to my side. I situate her in my lap with her back pressed to my chest, and grab the sponge from the ledge behind the tub. Gathering her hair, I drape it over the front of her left shoulder before I guide her head back onto mine. I love how she melts into me with a sigh, and I press a tender kiss to her right temple then seal it there with my cheek.

"Mmmm, you're spoiling me, Mr. Danvers," she says. "Keep it up, and I'll want this sort of treatment on a regular basis."

Her mouth is quirked up on one side, and I can tell she's trying to inject some humor, a defense mechanism for trying to open things up a minute ago. She probably expects me to jump at the chance to make a joke and erase any hint of seriousness. But having her in my arms like this, in my house, in my tub, makes me feel ten-fucking-feet tall, and I've decided that I like that feeling too much to go backward.

"Well, Ms. Wendall, you'll be happy to hear that I kind of like spoiling you, so anytime you want a milk bath and foot rub, you just say the words."

"Funny," she says, "but you actually sounded serious when you said that."

"I am serious." Soaking the sponge in the water, I run it up her right arm and then back down. Then I do the same to her left arm. When she still hasn't spoken, I try elaborating. "I know we agreed to no strings, and I think I speak for both of us when I say it's been fucking fantastic. But I don't know…" I shrug, moving her head in the process. "Now I'm thinking that maybe it doesn't have to be only about the sex."

"Meaning what, exactly?" she asks carefully.

I watch my hand as it drags the sponge over her clavicle and upper chest. "Meaning I like you, Jane. I like spending time with you whether I'm balls deep inside your tight little body or we're watching reruns of *The Dukes of Hazard* at two in the morning. So, I'd like to spend *more* time with you. Take you out on a real date to a restaurant that doesn't serve pancakes, or any other kind of breakfast food, so you're not reminded of work."

I take a moment to enjoy the light tinkling of laughter that escapes her as she opens her eyes and peers up at me through wet, spiky lashes. Damn, she's stunning. I abandon the sponge and bring my hand up to cup her jaw. "I want to be able to spend nights with you in my bed or me in yours. Doesn't have to be an every night thing, but I'd like the option, if that's something you'd be okay with."

"I'd be very okay with that," she whispers. "I really like you, too, Chance."

Jane smiles at me, full and wide, and I swear the room actually brightens. I told myself coming up here that I wasn't going to start anything with her—and I'm still not—but I need to kiss her more than I need my next breath right now, so I do. I lower my head the couple of inches and press my lips to hers.

That's when I feel her hand snake between our bodies and close around my cock.

Fuck. Me.

Chapter Seventeen

JANE

Chance *likes me*.

I have no idea how I got so lucky, but I'm not about to look a gift horse in the mouth, much less punch it, so I'm going to do the smart thing and take this one day at a time.

His thumb brushes over my cheek as his mouth descends and takes mine in a sensual kiss. Instantly, my body reacts. I feel my nipples pebble and my breasts grow heavy as I arch my back and they break the surface of the water. I move my right hand behind me and wrap it around Chance's hardening cock, needing him.

He groans at my touch, but then pulls my hand away and wraps me up with our arms, holding me tight against him. As he dips his face into the crook of my neck, I feel his chest expand with a deep breath before it shudders out on a long exhale. "I didn't bring you up here for that, sweetness."

I'm temporarily distracted from my mission by his use of the endearment. I've come to adore it, but the idea that it's something he uses without discernment causes a twinge of resentment each time he says it. "Is using nicknames like 'sweetness' a professional necessity so you don't accidentally call a woman by the wrong name?"

He raises his head and looks me in the eyes. "No. I'm always present enough in the moment to remember a woman's name—if nothing else, she deserves that from me—and I've never been one to use pet names. But somehow calling you 'sweetness' came naturally to me, Jane, and now your name is the only one I remember."

And with that, the last of my inner cynic swoons and faints dead away. I'm officially a goner for this man. I don't know how to respond without sounding like an emotional and much less eloquent Juliet to his badass Romeo, so I communicate with my hips and remind him of what we both want. He inhales sharply and presses his forehead to mine.

"You're making this awfully fucking difficult, Jane. I'm trying to be good. You're tired. I wanted to take care of you and tuck you into bed with me."

My heart swells at least three times its normal size. The fact that he's trying to abstain from sex—something he clearly wants, if the erection prodding my lower back is anything to go by (and it is)—to "take care of me" is the most romantic thing he could do right now. His actions are backing up his words, and that's something that means *a lot* to me.

Justin always claimed how important I was to him, but I was never a priority, a fact that was never more evident than the day he told me he was taking a job clear across the country, knowing full-well I couldn't leave Chicago until after I'd finished my degree. And it's not like it was even a *better* job. It was a lateral move to a company in Los Angeles where there was "better weather" and he could "finally learn how to surf."

The serious boyfriend before that left me "to focus on his

career," too, except I discovered that his career's name was Candy and she had fake DD boobs and a Brazilian butt lift. So, it's fair to say that I have issues when men I'm with choose other things (or women) over me.

It's why Chance's side job as a stripper-for-hire has started to really bother me. The stronger my feelings for him grow, the more I hate the thought of random women groping him as he pretends to seduce them with his mostly-naked body. And that makes me ill. It's similar to a woman worrying about her man cheating because she was once his mistress and knows there's a chance of history repeating itself. Chance and I got together because I was a client—albeit an unknowing one—so who's to say he won't meet another woman the same way?

I have to wonder why he still does the job at all. It's certainly not because he needs the money, and if he likes dancing that much, he could go to one of the city's dozens of clubs. Is it the female attention? The rush of hearing their outrageous reactions to every little thing he does? Are they able to give him something I can't, satisfy him in a way I never can?

These are the things running through my mind every time I know he's at a gig, and I can't even say anything about it because our sexual exclusivity has no bearing on the other aspects in our lives. At least it didn't. Now that we're moving from casual lovers to something a little more substantial, I have a feeling my insecurities will get worse, not better.

But the last thing I want to be is that girl who nags her man about things he's been doing since before they were together. And he doesn't deserve to have the sins of the men who came before him dumped on his doorstep. Just because my previous boyfriends chose other things over me doesn't mean that Chance will do the same.

That's why, though it's on a much smaller scale, Chance putting my immediate needs above his is a gesture that truly touches me. And that makes me want him *actually* touching me all the more.

"You *have* taken care of me, and I loved it," I say, turning my face to place a kiss on his forehead. "But now I want to take care of each other."

Since my arms are pinned across my body under his, I rock my hips back to grind my ass at the base of his shaft. His breath hisses out through clenched teeth, and I know I'm wearing him down. He's a healthy, red-blooded male. He can only say no to sex for so long before he caves.

Twisting in his arms, I force him to loosen his hold, and turn to straddle his lap. There's plenty of room for my bent legs to rest on the outside of his, and I realize for the first time how roomy the tub really is. "This bathtub is magnificent, Chance. I've never seen a claw-foot tub this big before."

"I had it custom made. Standard sizes are too small for a guy my size. I look like a giant with my knees in my chest."

That image has me chuckling as I wrap my arms around his neck. "Well, I'm thankful it's big enough for the both of us."

Chance scoffed. "You don't take up much room, sweetness. In case you haven't noticed, you're a tiny little thing."

I gasp, feigning indignation. "Am not."

"Are, too," he says, smiling and leaning in for a kiss.

I'm sure he meant it to be innocent, a quick peck and then start to pull away. But I follow him back and nip his full lower lip before soothing the sting with a lick. Groaning, he grants me entry into his mouth, and I don't waste the falter in his resolve. I sweep in and dance my tongue with his. He tastes like beer and spearmint and *him*.

His arms band around my back and crush my breasts against the hard planes of his chest. I roll my hips forward, desperate for the connection he's denying us. He wrenches his mouth away so I take my kissing show on the road and attack his jawline, his neck.

"We should get out," he says, his voice strained. I hum my disagreement as I kiss the soft spot behind his ear. I want him like this. Now, here. "I'd rather take you to bed so I can make love to you properly."

I pull back and search his face for clues that he actually said two particular words. "Make love?"

"Yeah, make love," he repeats, a hint of amusement playing at the corners of his mouth. "We don't always have to play rough, do we?"

"Not at all. It's just I didn't think…I mean, I thought you were only into…" I shake my head and tell myself to quit while I'm ahead. "Never mind."

His expression turns solemn. "That used to be the case, but now…" He reaches up and strokes my cheek with the backs of his fingers. "Now I'm into everything, as long as it's with you."

My jaw falls slack with the intention of responding, but words fail me. His brow furrows the slightest bit, a wrinkle of doubt marring his smooth skin. "I'd never do anything to hurt you, Jane. You know that, don't you?"

I might not know everything about Chance Danvers, but I do know he'd never do anything to physically hurt me. Everything we've ever done together has been about mutual pleasure, even when it comes from a little bit of pain. I trust this man implicitly with my body.

But as I gaze into the deep blue of his eyes, and see the tender way they roam over my face as he waits for my answer, it's not my body I'm worried about. Chance is showing me a side of himself that could very well destroy me if I let myself fall for him. Because eventually he'll want his freedom, and all I'll want is him.

I'd do well to keep that in the forefront of my mind, to build some walls around my heart to protect it from the storm my brain can see coming from a mile away. Except, people who build walls never actually *feel* anything. They experience things in half-truths, as mere shadows of what they're meant to be. And as much as I'm afraid of the falling out I'm sure will come, I'm even more afraid of missing out on the rush of falling *in*.

"Yes, I know that," I whisper, giving him a soft smile. "Make love to me, Chance. Right here, just like this." I raise up and position the head of him at my entrance, then he sucks in a breath and holds it as I slowly impale myself on his thick cock.

As always, I'm overwhelmed by the way he stretches me to fit him, my channel molding around his hard shaft so that it caresses every one of my nerves. And yet, this feels different. This isn't our usual fucking. There's no roughness, no hints of humiliation. No dominance or submission. He isn't only filling me up in the physical sense. As I stare into those fathomless blue pools, I feel him pouring himself into a void in my heart I hadn't even known was there.

"God, Jane," he says when I'm fully seated. "You feel…" I rock my hips. "*Fuck*."

"Good?"

He shakes his head almost imperceptibly, as though he doesn't know how to answer, then grabs the sides of my head and takes my mouth in a soul-stealing kiss. It isn't fast or hurried, but is no less intense for it. Without words, our bodies speak about things our heads won't allow and our hearts will only half believe.

As our tongues thrust against one another, Chance's hands grip the globes of my ass and guide my movements. Breaking the kiss, he encourages me. "That's it, baby. Work yourself on my dick. This is all you. Take what you need from me."

Slow and steady, I grind myself on him in fluid strokes.

Back and forth, in mini circles, up and down, I do it all. He groans and cusses. His hands roam over my body, hefting the weight of my breasts, tweaking my nipples then sucking them into his mouth.

The sparks in my belly have turned into an all-out conflagration of desire, sending invisible waves of heat rippling under the surface of my skin as my climax grows nearer. My motions pick up speed, and I'm racing toward the finish and the high I know awaits me at the end, yet still never wanting to stop, never wanting this amazing feeling to get away, in case I never get this opportunity again.

"You're so sexy, Jane, you know that? And beautiful. So goddamn beautiful it hurts."

"Oh God, Chance, I…I'm…"

"Fuck, you're getting tighter. Don't stop," he grinds out, then reaches down to rub my swollen clit. "Keep going, baby. I want you squeezing my cock when I come."

"*Yessssss…*" White light eclipses my vision, and I give a keening cry as my orgasm finally crests, atomizing into a million specks of pleasure that flood my body.

He pumps once, twice, and the third time he holds and shudders his release, roaring into the side of my neck as he spills himself inside me. I hold on to him tightly, and my limbs tremble as he rocks us through the last of the aftershocks.

I don't know how long we sit like that, fused together, but the water is barely lukewarm when he finally lifts his head. His cheeks are flushed, his lips swollen from our kisses. Unable to resist, I run my fingers through his damp locks, pushing them back from his face and letting my nails lightly trail over his scalp.

I discovered how much he likes that a few days ago, and now I love doing it whenever I can. I love watching his eyes close and his head drop back onto his shoulders as the shivers roll through him. I love that I can do something so innocent that gives him just as visceral a reaction as when we're doing much less innocent things.

I take advantage and lean in to dust kisses under his stubbly jawline, causing him to groan and press his forehead to mine. "Are you trying to kill me, woman?"

I smile coyly and draw designs through the trim hair on his muscular chest. "That depends," I say. "Would another go-round kill you?"

His quiet laugh comes from deep in his chest, and I can feel the vibrations in my fingertips. "Definitely not. But even if it did," he says as he traces my lower lip, "it'd be worth it."

I still, taking in his words and the way his eyes are boring into mine, and tell myself not to look too much into them. Sexually, we're great together, neither of us has ever denied that, and that's exactly what he probably meant. He certainly couldn't mean that making love to me was far more necessary than he'd thought possible.

Though, if I let myself reflect on things too closely, I might come to that conclusion myself and realize that I'd fallen fast and hard for my handyman stripper.

A chill races over my skin, and he immediately snaps out of Flirty Chance and back into caretaker mode. "Come on, sweetness, let's get you warmed up and into bed. Round two can wait until you've had some rest."

Tired and sated, I let him lift me from the tub and dry me off with a towel that had been hanging on a warming rack. It's like wrapping up in a blanket that just came out of a hot dryer and has now ruined me for all future post-bathing ventures, as did noticing his multi-showerhead marble shower stall with bench seat. I seriously do want to move into Chance's master bathroom.

When he picks me up, the independent feminist in me is ready with an "I can walk" protest. But as soon as I'm cradled against him, my arms instinctively go around his neck, and I press my cheek onto his shoulder, quickly shutting the bitch up. I can walk some other damn time.

He sets me in the middle of his luxuriously unmade bed—which makes me feel better about my own perpetually rumpled bed—and gets in as he pulls the covers around us. Romeo hops up from wherever he was on the floor and, after several turns in place, curls into a little ball on the side we're not using. Chuckling, I give him a couple of scratches behind his ears, then sigh in contentment as I sink into the mattress that probably costs more than half a year's rent at my apartment.

But it isn't until Chance tunnels an arm under my head and wraps the other one around my middle to tuck me into his chest that I know what true contentment is. I feel a tender kiss at my temple, and as my breathing evens out, and exhaustion finally tugs me into the shadows of my mind, I hear echoes of a whisper I can't be sure came from reality and not the beginning of a dream.

"I more than like you, Jane. A *lot* more. And it's scaring the hell out of me."

That makes two of us…

Chapter Eighteen

JANE

I wasn't able to get off early from my shift at the restaurant, so I arrive at my aunt's house in Elmhurst about an hour after the party starts. My cousin Julia turned twenty-one today so my aunt is throwing her a huge birthday party combined with one of those pleasure party events, where a representative shows up with a bag full of sex toys to demonstrate and samples of edible lube to pass around for everyone to try. Needless to say, my aunt—my dad's sister—has always been the coolest mom I've ever known. My own mom is great, too, but she's more "lemonades and family picnics" than "margaritas and sex parties."

I can hear the squeals and laughter from all the way out on the street as I make my way up the sidewalk to the front door. My smile comes easy, as I've been on cloud nine for the last couple of weeks. Chance and I have been great. Better than great. Most weeknights he spends at my place, and then we spend the weekends at his.

Yesterday, I finally turned in my thesis, and he took me out to celebrate. We went to dinner at the Signature Room on the ninety-sixth floor of the John Hancock building and then hung out at Navy Pier and rode the Ferris wheel (where he may or may not have made me come with his hand up my dress).

All in all, I couldn't be happier, and as much fun as I know I'll have at Julia's party, I can't wait to see Chance later. He's coming to my place, since he's in my area of the city for a job, and then he's teaching me how to make microwavable s'mores—a bachelor staple according to him—and we'll watch the new Jason Statham movie. I gave him my spare key since I figured I'd be here pretty late, but maybe I can sneak out early without anyone noticing.

I let myself in, and I'm instantly bombarded with loud music, colored lights, and the smell of alcohol. It's like stepping into a nightclub in the middle of a suburban home. The foyer is empty, and from the excited sounds coming from the back of the house, I'm assuming everyone is in the family room.

"Oh my God, Janey, you're finally here!"

I turn to the right, where the dining room table is covered in enough bottles of liquor to serve an army of drunks for a week, and see Emily, Julia's older sister. It's obvious she's had a few already when she bum-rushes me in a hug that almost has us falling on our asses. Luckily, I'm sober and able to steady us before we need an ambulance.

"Hey, Em," I say, returning her hug before peeling her off. "Sorry I'm late."

"Don't be silly, you're right on time. Wow, you look fantastic. Have you been working out?"

Only if you count the calories burned by having tons of sex. "No, but I tried a new makeup technique. I found a smoky eye tutorial on YouTube that doesn't make me look like a raccoon," I say with a wink.

She shakes her head. "No, it's something else. I mean, your eyes look amazing, but…" She gasps and points at me accusingly. "Oh my God, you're totally getting laid!"

I laugh and try to deny it, but I can feel the heat in my face making me a liar. "Okay, fine," I admit, "I *might* have a pretty awesome thing going with a guy right now, but that's all you're getting out of me."

"I knew it! I'm so happy for you, Janey. You deserve something awesome after that last prick. It's about time you hopped back on the horse."

Before Emily gets any more preachy, I change the subject. "How's the birthday girl?"

"Fantastic and very, very drunk. Come on, let's get you a drink and then you have to see what I got her. Hands down, it's the best present here."

"Okay, but only one drink," I say as she pushes me into the dining room. "I drove and I can only stay for a couple of hours."

She stops in the middle of pouring me a partially liquefied frozen margarita from the blender and looks at me like I just told her Santa isn't coming this year. "Whaaaaaat? Janey, come on, why do you have to leave so early? You just *got* here."

Thank you, Captain Obvious. I sigh dramatically and say, "I know, it totally sucks, but I have to be at work at three a.m."—(no, I don't)—"and I need at least a few hours of sleep if I hope to not pour coffee into anyone's lap."

My cousin makes a sound of disgust, but resumes pouring my drink. "When are you going to stop working your entire life away?"

"As soon as I can afford to. Tell you what, the day I can quit waitressing to supplement my income, you and Aunt Martha can throw me a party from dusk till dawn, just like this one, if you want."

Her face lights up as she hands me the strawberry margarita. Clapping, she says, "Deal! And I'll get you the same gift I got Julia."

I laugh at her drunk-girl enthusiasm. "What is this amazing gift you keep talking about?" A chorus of excited screams rends the air, and I have to shout to be heard. "And what the hell is going on back there?"

"It's my present to Julia! Come on, we're missing out on all the fun," she yells over the din and leads the way through the house to the great room in the back.

All I can see are the backs of women standing in a circle and cheering, and I half wonder if Aunt Martha hasn't erected a Jell-O ring where naked men fight to the gelatin death. As crazy as it sounds, it's not outside the realm of possibilities when it comes to my aunt.

Emily grabs my hand and pushes her way through the crowd, dragging me with her as I try not to spill my filled-to-the-brim drink. When we break through the other side, I'm shocked at how many people are actually here. There have to be at least fifty women ranging in their early twenties to late fifties around the perimeter of the room, some sitting on furniture and folding chairs with the rest standing to fill in the gaps.

It's when my eyes land on a practically naked Austin that my stomach drops out. He singles out one of the squealing girls and sits her on the tufted square ottoman in the middle of the circle.

Emily leans in and squeals in my ear. "Strippers! Told you it's the best gift ever. I saw these guys at a party I was at last month, and knew I had to get them for tonight. Are they not the hottest specimens you've ever seen?"

I'm unable to speak around the lump of nerves in my throat, but Em just laughs, probably thinking I'm struck dumb by the drool factor of her surprise. I nervously look around the room, searching for Chance. My heart stops when the crowd parts on the other side, but it picks up again when it ends up being a tattooed guy leading a second girl into the circle. As he places her identically on the other side of the ottoman, I recognize the man as Roman. At least, I *think* it's Roman.

Every time I've seen the straight-laced lawyer, he's dressed either in a suit or preppy casual wear you'd see in an Eddie Bauer catalog, the perfect picture of money and sophistication.

But *this* Roman is like the other one's evil twin. His jet-black hair is sticking up like fingers have been plowing through it, diamond studs are in his earlobes, and tattoos cover almost every inch of his upper body and arms. As he and Austin start dancing for their captive audience of two, Roman sticks his tongue out, revealing a silver ball flashing in the lights. His ears *and* his tongue are pierced? I briefly wonder what else might be pierced, but stop myself before my eyes drop to the front of his thin, white boxer briefs.

One thing is for sure, though. Roman isn't the model country-club boy I'd originally thought. He's the poster child for wild times and probably even wilder sex. Addison would eat him up and lick the plate clean.

As they start dancing, relief that Austin and Roman are the only two men here floods my veins. I don't think I'd handle it well to see Chance getting pawed by other women. Taking several sips of my fruity drink, I decide to relax and enjoy the show along with the rest of the crowd. Despite not doing anything for me, Chance's friends are still fine specimens of the male form and dance like Channing Tatum.

The guys step up onto the ottoman with their feet on either side of their respective girls. They're both so tall that the girls have to look up to get an eyeful of what the men are packing, but then the problem is rectified when Austin and Roman clasp their right hands together and lean back, using each other for counter balance. They bend their knees to bring their crotches eye-level, then use their free hands at the backs of the girls' heads to pull them in close and grind on their faces.

Both of the girls' hands go to the men's butts, grabbing and squeezing, and the crowd goes absolutely nuts. I laugh and shake my head as the guys eat up the reaction then jump down simultaneously. Their moves are so in sync, I wonder how many times they've done this exact routine. They each kiss the girls on the cheeks and then lead them back to their places in the circle before making the universal sign with their hands for the room to quiet down.

Austin, who's wearing red boxer briefs with a yellow waistband and reads "Today I'm Your Fireman" on the ass, points to my cousin in her birthday tiara and sash. "It's time for the birthday girl to get her birthday treat. Come here, darlin.'"

Again, the women cheer and get rowdy as Austin leads Julia center stage and sits her down on the ottoman.

Roman heads to the fireplace mantle where his phone and a speaker are set up like the one Chance has. For as small as those things are, they pump out dance club quality sound. He chooses something from a playlist and a new song starts up, all sexy bass and syncopated rhythms. The guys approach Julia and each straddle one of her legs as they perform body rolls so fluid they look virtually boneless.

Suddenly the music starts skipping like it's a scratched CD instead of a digitally mastered track playing from a smartphone, then it stops altogether. Boos rise up from the peanut gallery and Roman and Austin look at each other like they're not sure what to do, but Austin manages to calm the masses in a matter of seconds.

"Ladies, ladies, it's okay, we know what to do." He looks at Roman and says, "Ruthless, whenever we need something fixed, what do we do?"

A devilish grin turns Roman—aka Ruthless—into a wicked panty-melter. "That's easy. We call *the handyman*."

Screams erupt in stereo, and I'm positive I've lost fifty percent of my hearing. *Oh, God…no no no n—*

"Ladies, put your hands together for *Romeo* the *Handyman*!"

The crowd parts to my left, and in struts the man I've been seeing, wearing the same coveralls he wore the first night we met. The women are going crazy, and the lust-struck look on my cousin's face says she'd like to explore my boyfriend with nothing more than her tongue.

For the next bit of eternity, I watch with acid churning in my gut as Chance dances and methodically reveals more and more of his hard body while Julia rubs him down like her very life depends on mapping out his muscles. His damp hair started off pulled back in a low pony, but he's since ripped out the hair tie and now his shoulder-length locks are whipping across his face, adding another level of sexy to the already edible package.

I want to get drunk and make myself numb against the jealousy and angry proprietary feelings clawing at my insides. I hate that I feel this way. This is his *job*—or one of them, at least. I've known all along that this is what he does sometimes on the weekends; it's not like he's been dishonest or kept this a secret. It's how I *met* him, for Christ's sake.

Down to only a small pair of blue boxer briefs with white handprints on the ass, Chance uncrosses Julia's legs and yanks her butt to the edge of the ottoman. Standing to the right of her, he bends to the left, placing his left shoulder on her left thigh with his head going between her thighs. Then he pushes himself into a handstand, his shoulders braced on her thighs. His line of sight right now is straight up my cousin's skirt while he spreads his legs and gyrates his pelvis directly in front of her face.

Julia wears a look of awe and actually goes to *grab* my man's cock. I'm torn between throwing up where I stand and breaking my cousin's fingers one by one. I'm spared from doing either when Chance avoids her molestation, just barely, by rotating out of the position until he's standing again.

But the dance isn't over, and though I doubt it'll get much worse than what he's already done, I can't continue to watch or I *will* do something to cause a scene. I lean over to Emily, who's still next to me, and yell directly into her ear so she can hear me. I make an excuse about the drink not sitting well and ask her to tell Julia I wish her the best.

Just as I turn to leave, Austin tosses two cans of whipped cream to Chance, two to Roman, and grabs two for himself. I watch in wide-eyed horror as each of them make designs on their bodies with the fluffy dessert topping and offer to let a woman—in Chance's case, Julia—lick it off.

As I push through the crowd and make my way out of the house, I realize I was wrong: things are *definitely* getting much worse.

Chapter Nineteen

The night is hot and humid, adding to the sticky feeling already coating my body from the P4H job I'm coming from. The guys and I used baby wipes to do a preliminary cleaning before getting dressed to leave, but I need a proper shower to wash off the whipped cream, sweat, and dozens of touches that aren't my girl's.

I can't wait to see her tonight. She said she had to go to her aunt's house for her cousin's birthday. We figured out our schedules, and she'll probably be back about an hour after me, so she gave me her spare key to let myself in. I'll have plenty of time to shower and set things up for our S'mores 'n' Statham night.

I grab the bag of food supplies from the passenger seat of my truck and bound up her apartment building's stairs two at a time. I use the key to let myself in and I'm locking up behind me when I hear noises coming from the kitchen. Loud noises.

Rounding the corner, I'm surprised to find Jane opening

up cabinet doors and slamming them shut. She's obviously looking for something and is getting frustrated at not finding it. Not wanting to scare the shit out of her, I rustle the plastic bag as a subtle warning, then say, "Hey, sweetness."

She jumps and spins, white-knuckling the edge of the counter behind her. "Fuck, Chance, don't do that!"

So much for not scaring the shit out of her. I chuckle and set the bag on the counter. "Sorry, baby, I tried not to startle you. What are you doing in here, anyway? You look upset."

Sighing she brings her hands up and pushes her hair back from her face. "I can't find my chamomile tea. I used to drink it when I needed to relax, and I'd really like to relax right now, but I can't fricking find it. It used to be in this cabinet, but now I don't know where it is."

When she opens the cabinet door, I spot the box of tea immediately. It's on the top shelf, pushed all the way to the back where the short-stack can't see it. "Found it," I say, easily retrieving it for her. She mumbles a thanks and moves to fill the kettle with water. "Have a bad day, babe? Did you not go to your cousin's thing?"

Jane sets the kettle on the stove a little harder than seems necessary and turns the burner on high. "No, I went, but I didn't stay long. Wasn't my scene."

I want to wrap my arms around her, comfort her until whatever's bothering her goes away, but I really need to bathe before that because I'm gross. "Not your scene?" I ask. "I thought you said it was at your aunt's house."

"It was," she says, turning to face me. "But my aunt isn't your typical parent who invites the family over for cake and ice cream and gives her daughters nice sweater sets."

I arch a brow in question and start taking the ingredients I'd picked up for s'mores out of the bag. "Then what type of parent is she?"

"The type who turns her suburban Elmhurst home into

a night club with enough alcohol to warrant a liquor license, invites a sex toy rep to bring samples of her latest and greatest, and hires male entertainers who cover themselves in whipped cream as the highlight of the evening."

I freeze, the bag of marshmallows mid-transfer, and look over at Jane, who's leaning back on the counter with her arms hugging her middle as she chews on her lower lip. Ah, fuck me, this isn't good.

"Julia is your cousin." She nods. "And you saw me dance for her?"

She snorts. "I think you mean *on* her."

Shitdamnfuck. "Baby, you know that doesn't mean anything. It's all an act."

Again she nods. "I know that. I mean, logically I know, but it really sucked actually seeing it. I love my cousin, but I wanted to rip her hair out by the roots every time she touched you."

Part of me likes how jealous she is, and that part of me wants to smile and laugh at how cute she looks as she tries not to pout about another woman touching me. "I'm sorry it sucked, but it's just a job. You're the one I'm coming home to at night, as evidenced by my presence right now. I'm here with you, Jane, not anyone else."

Her teeth are still worrying her lip, which has *me* worried. If she doesn't stop, she might break the skin. Fuck the state of my hygiene; I need to kiss her.

Closing the small distance, I hold her face in my hands and spare her lip by molding mine around it. For a second, she melts into me, just as she always does, but then I feel her hands on my chest, and she pushes me away.

"Sorry, but you smell like her," she says, wiping her mouth with the back of her wrist. "My cousin has worn Escape by Calvin Klein since the tenth grade, and I can smell it on you."

Shit, I was so worried about the sweat and whipped

cream that I forgot about the female scents I come away with after having rubbed up against them. Slick move, asshole. I apologize and take a couple of steps back, ready to tell her I'll be back in five minutes, after I've showered, when she says the one thing I never wanted to hear her ask.

"Have you ever given any thought to not stripping anymore?"

Jesus Christ, this is like Sandra all over again. It's the question that marks the beginning of the end. Sandra had given me an ultimatum. Either I stop stripping, or she was stopping the engagement. I didn't stop stripping.

"Nope," I say, trying to tamp down the flames of aggravation. "I haven't."

"Okay," she draws out slowly. "Well, is it something you'd consider giving thought to?"

Planting my feet, I cross my arms over my chest. "I gotta say, I honestly didn't expect this from you. I thought it didn't bother you, that you were more mature than this."

She folds her arms, too, and narrows her eyes slightly. "Chance, don't be an ass, and don't make this about me."

"What do you mean don't make this about you? You couldn't handle watching me dance for other women, so now you want me to stop. But I'll tell you how we fix that. We make sure I'm never working any party you're attending. Problem solved."

Jane throws her hands up and lets them drop to slap on her legs. "Yes, fine. The part about me hating to see other women paw at you is about me. But this is deeper than that. I mean, what is it about stripping that's so important to you? It's not like you need the money anymore. Do you get a rush from being a sex symbol, being objectified by strange women? What?"

"Don't start shrinking me with your social worker thesis shit, Jane," I say angrily. "I'm not one of your case studies, and I don't have any issues from my childhood driving my behavior."

"I didn't say that. I'm just trying to understand why it's so important to you. Am I not enough for you?"

"*Now* who's making this about you?" I say, seething and turning her own words against her. See? All women want to change the man they're with. It's a fact of life. Inevitable. Women are inherent fixers of the "broken boy." But I'm not. Fucking. Broken. "Bottom line, I don't have one damn reason to stop. I was doing this long before you came along, and I'll still be doing it after we're done."

Jane rears her head back like I just slapped her. Subconsciously—or, hell, maybe even consciously—I chose those words to deliberately hurt her, because she was damn sure hurting me. I was so stupid for thinking this time would be different. That *she* was different. But in the end, she wants me to be someone I'm not, and that doesn't wash with me.

"I see." She wraps her arms around her middle again, hugging herself against the pain swimming in her eyes. "Then I guess there's also no reason to prolong our inevitable split. Please leave, Chance."

I force my hand to get her key from my pocket. I slap it onto the counter, causing her to flinch. "Thanks for the reminder of why I enjoy being single, Jane."

I stride out of the kitchen toward the front door. I hear the tea kettle start to scream, much like the voice in my head is screaming at me to go back and figure out a way to fix this. But there's no point. I can't.

As good as I am, this is one situation that not even this handyman can fix.

Chapter Twenty

CHANCE

"So what do you think are our chances of retaining tonight's business, Danvers?"

Roman's joke pulls a half-hearted chuckle from me before I take several long pulls on my beer. The guys and I decided to go out when our gig at a bachelorette party got cut short. Apparently the bride-to-be had promised her very religious fiancé there would be no strippers in attendance, but the don't-give-a-shit maid-of-honor made no such promises and decided to give her sister a last night of freedom she'd never forget.

That, of course, caused some problems when the soon-to-be groom decided he had to see her one last time before the midnight deadline of their wedding day and walked in on O'Donnell thrusting his junk in her face as he braced himself over her on the living room floor.

"I think that despite the high level of customer satisfaction," I say, "we probably won't be getting the future

Mrs. Carter's business anytime soon."

Austin, Roman, and Liam all laugh and clink their beer bottles together in a toast to customer satisfaction. I signal to a waitress for another round for the table, then drain the rest of my fourth Corona. If the night goes well, I'll get a dozen or so under my belt before Austin drops me off at home. That way I'll be too drunk to lie awake and think of Jane, a problem I've been having every fucking night for the last two weeks, ever since I walked out of her apartment.

"We might not get the new bride's repeat business, but her sister was smokin' hot and ready to go." Austin holds up his one and only beer and lifts a finger from the bottle to point at no one in particular. "I would've gotten a bonus dance out of that one, for sure. She practically blew me through my skivvies in the middle of the party. I think she would've been down to let you in on the fun, too, Reeves."

"I think you're right," Roman says. "Too bad she had to stay and play referee for Big Sis. That dude was furious. I wonder if he'll call off the wedding."

Liam slaps the table. "Damn, that means my thrusting game would be the reason a marriage gets called off." He shakes his head and whistles. "That's pretty fucking heavy, man, but I guess what they say is true. With great cock comes great responsibility."

Everyone laughs and makes the obligatory dick jokes at O'Donnell's expense. Everyone except me. I'm not in a laughing mood lately, and not only that, I can sympathize with the Carter guy 100 percent.

Austin passes around the bottles that the waitress brought over to those of us having another. "It's a good thing we have our anonymity, because the way that guy was acting, it wouldn't surprise me if he made a hunting party out of his groomsmen and tracked us down."

I use the edge of the table to pop off the cap on my beer

and take a long pull before finally putting my two cents in. "Can you honestly blame the man, Massey?" I realize my rhetorical question comes out more like a growl, but I don't bother checking my attitude. "How would you have felt in his shoes? I'll tell you one thing, if that was me walking in on some asshole grinding his junk in Jane's face, the man's privates would become his 'publics' when I ripped them off and chucked them into the goddamn street."

All three of my friends fall silent and stare at me with varied expressions that all communicate the same message: *No shit, Sherlock.*

That's when two things dawn on me. One, I'm in love with Jane Wendall. And two, Jane's reaction the night of her cousin's party was completely valid. Because she loves me, too.

"Ah, fuck." I shove my fingers through my hair and pull at the scalp, hoping the physical pain on the outside will somehow alleviate the emotional shit strangling me on the inside.

"It's about time you caught on, brother." This from Roman, who claps a hand on my shoulder and squeezes. "Now that you have, how do you want to get her back? Massey and I have a couple of ideas, if you want to hear them."

Austin perks up. "My favorite is the one with you in a banana hammock using a can of whipped cream, sliced bananas, and a monkey."

I don't even have the focus to appreciate what a fucking moronic idea that must be because I'm too busy shutting down my newfound hope. "It doesn't matter how I feel about her. She wants to change me, just like Sandra."

"For as smart as you are," Roman says, "you can be such a fucking moron. Sandy never loved you. When you guys met, dating a stripper was the perfect way of rebelling against her father."

"Yeah, man, she loved using you to pick fights with him," Austin says, chiming in. "But once she grew out of that phase, then it was all about provin' Daddy wrong and gettin' you to fit in with the richy-rich folks at their yacht club. You were like a pet project."

"Fuck, dude." Liam shakes his head with a solemn expression. "I didn't know you back then, so I can't speak about your ex. But if a chick told me right now to stop working at P4H—to stop the job that I love doing, and that's building up my savings for when I graduate—I'd tell her to take a hike."

I slap the table in front of me and sit up straight. "See? That's what I'm talking about. Thank you, O'Donnell."

"Don't thank me, boss. I'm talking about being twenty-three and still loving the life of a college idiot and stripper-for-hire. You guys all started this business when you were where I'm at now, but that was what, five plus years ago? Now you're established in life and the owner of a major construction company.

"Being a stripper isn't who you are anymore, man. It's just something you still do on the side. Whether it's because you enjoy the dancing, the women, or just want to hold on to your misspent youth, I don't know. But what I do know, is that if I were in *your* shoes," he says with emphasis to call back to my remark earlier, "and I had a girl like Jane who wanted me all to herself, you can bet your ass I'd never be shaking mine for another woman ever again."

As though punctuating his monologue, he takes the last drink of his beer and slams his empty on the table. "I'm out, fellas. I've got a shit ton of homework this weekend, so I might as well use this time to get a jump on it. Good luck, man, and thanks for the drinks."

Roman and Austin raise their beers in the kid's direction and I do the same, though I'm acting on autopilot.

"Well, how 'bout that?" Austin says after Liam is gone. "Who knew O'Donnell was such a fount of wisdom?"

I don't answer. I'm trying to process everything the guys said, but this fifth beer is making things move a shit ton slower in the old gray matter. My friends aren't wrong about Sandra. I realized after I broke things off that her motivations for being with me weren't so much about love as they were about her ongoing feud with her father. Which only solidified my tenet of never letting a woman change me. But Liam's little diatribe poses a new question: who, exactly, am I?

Certainly not the same kid who started this venture with his buddies in college. Not even the same guy who mistook an infatuation with a woman I believed to be out of my league for real love. Hell, I'm not even the same guy I was a few months ago before I met Jane. Since finding her, things I used to find pleasure in—partying on the weekends till all hours of the morning, getting mauled by strange women, the random hookups…none of it interests me anymore.

I'm still working the P4H jobs, but if I'm honest with myself, my heart isn't in it. Even when Jane and I were together, I was anxious to get through the gigs so I could see her.

I make sure to put on a good show and fake my way through it, but every time another woman touches me, I'm picturing Jane; remembering how good it felt when her delicate hands roamed over my body and her nails scored my skin.

Somewhere along the line, being a stripper-for-hire stopped being about getting paid to have fun and became more of a chore. So what the hell am I giving up by staying behind the scenes and not stripping anymore?

The answer? Not a goddamn thing. I'd actually be *gaining* free time. Time I could be spending with the woman I love… with Jane.

Roman places his forearms on the table and leans in, narrowing his eyes on me like he's about to cross-examine me on the witness stand. "I'm curious. Did Jane really say that you have to quit?"

"I know what she was getting at. I'm not stupid."

"That's debatable," he counters, "but you're sidestepping the question. Think back, Danvers, because I'm willing to bet she never actually made a demand on you."

Roman's confidence gives me pause. My eyebrows draw together in concentration as I search the memory for the words that will vindicate my actions that night, even if I've since decided to give her what she wants for reasons of my own.

Have you ever given any thought to not stripping anymore?
I'm just trying to understand why it's so important to you.

She'd said a few other things, but those two lines pretty much summed up her half of the conversation. Jane never intended to give me an ultimatum or wanted to change me. She'd been bothered by what she'd seen—understandably so, considering I turn murderous at the thought of the situation being reversed—and wanted to talk about it. But what did *I* do? I'd jumped to conclusions, said hurtful things I didn't mean, and ruined everything.

Fuck me. I'm an asshole.

My little *aha* moment must be showing on my face because Roman takes the opportunity to make his closing statement. "That's what I thought," he says, sitting back. "And if that doesn't tell you what kind of person she is, brother, I don't know what will."

The realization lifts the ten-ton weight I've been carrying around since walking out of Jane's apartment that night. Roman and Austin clink their bottlenecks like a congratulating fist bump for making the town idiot see the light, and I can't even be offended because they're right about everything. What pisses me off is that deep down I knew all of this, but I kept it buried beneath the fear of the past repeating itself, the fear of not being enough for Jane.

But no more. It's time to step up and be the man she needs me to be. To own up to my mistakes, tell her how much I love her.

Austin's eyes light up with childlike excitement as he rubs his hands together. "Now we work on getting her back. What's it gonna be, boys?"

That's a good question. I'm ready to do whatever it takes to convince her to let me back in, but something tells me talking isn't going to be enough. I hurt her. I essentially chose something else over her, just like the fuckwads in her past did. I need to remind her that what we have together is different—*better*—from what she'll have with any other man. That I know her and love her in ways no other man will ever understand.

Only me.

"Guys," I say, getting their attention. "I appreciate your offer to help, but you'll have to save your banana hammock and monkey idea for another time. I know exactly what I have to do."

By now, she'll have erected thick walls to protect her heart against further pain. I'll have to push her mentally to the one place she always listens to me—to the one place I've never broken her trust. And to do that, I'll have to push her *physically*, and make her body listen to me first.

Chapter Twenty-One

JANE

Getting your heart broken sucks. Even worse is when you break it your-damn-self. Standing in the steamy bathroom after my shower, I stare at my wavy reflection in the condensation-coated mirror and gingerly rub the area that hides the tattered pieces just beneath the surface. Absently, I marvel at how healthy someone can appear on the outside when everything that matters has been decimated on the inside.

It's been weeks since Chance and I stopped seeing each other. What I felt when Justin left me was a minor nuisance compared to this soul-numbing ache in my chest. The daily reminder that Chance is no longer mine hurts with an intensity I can't describe. So many times I picked up my phone to call him, to tell him that I'm sorry and that the stripping isn't a big deal—that it doesn't matter as long as I can have him back.

But in the end, I forced myself to put down the phone. That night, I'd only wanted to have a conversation—to try and understand why dancing naked for strangers was so essential to him—and he'd blown it off like my feelings were of little consequence. It doesn't matter if I've since decided it's something I could learn to live with as long as I know he's faithful and comes home to me afterward. That he was so quick to dismiss what we had as merely temporary tells me that I was invested, mentally and emotionally, way more than he ever was. Which means eventually he'd end up choosing something else over me. Even if that something else was as simple as freedom.

I'm tired of coming in second place. I deserve to be *first*, goddamn it, and if nothing else, I'm proud of myself for finally sticking to my guns on this all-important issue. Unfortunately, gaining a newfound confidence and sense of self-worth doesn't mean this still doesn't hurt like a bitch.

I miss him so damn much. I've actually found myself wishing he worked in a strip club where I could sit in the shadows and watch him dance. I wouldn't love seeing random skanks pawing at him like he's the second coming of Christ for the sexual revolution, but I'd suck it up if it meant I got to see him even from a distance. I'd tune out everyone else in the club and pretend he was dancing for me.

Only me.

After running a towel over my wet hair, I pull on a baby tee and pair of boy shorts for makeshift pajamas, then shrug on my robe and shuffle out to the couch for my nightly Mopey Bitch routine. I curl up into the corner, hug my knees to my chest, and rest my cheek along the back cushion where he used to sit. I don't know if traces of his scent still linger in the upholstery or if I'm merely imagining it. Honestly, I don't care if it is my mind playing tricks on me as long as I get to smell him.

My apartment is silent with the exception of the steady ticking of the wall clock and the thunderous rumble of memories in my head. Each click of the second hand sounds like another nail being hammered into the coffin of mental self-torture I've laid myself in. God, this sucks. Like, really, *really* sucks. But it'll get better, right? They say time heals all wounds, so *eventually* this pain will have to lessen. I don't even want to think about the alternative. It has to get better…

My eyes shoot open to the sound of someone pounding on my door. I glance in confusion at the pitch-black world outside my window, then to the clock that reads two-thirty, made visible by the low light of the nearby table lamp. I must have fallen asleep—

More pounding startles me back to the present and turns my stomach inside out. There's only one person who's ever demanded entry at this hour. One person who's ever used the side of his fist like a jackhammer trying to splinter the offensive barrier between us.

"*Jane*. Open this goddamn door before I break it the fuck down."

"Holy shit," I whisper into the darkness. Before I comprehend my movement, I find myself at the door, sliding the chain lock out and twisting the deadbolt. I don't even get the chance to touch the doorknob before it turns. I have to jump back as the door swings open to allow Chance inside, then he kicks it closed behind him.

My breath catches as I take him in—tall and muscular and so fucking sexy it almost hurts to look. He's dressed in his favorite pair of faded jeans and a plain white T-shirt that hugs his body and makes my mouth water. Like the first time I saw him, he reminds me of Thor, the god of thunder, with his hair hanging loose around his shoulders and the powerful intensity vibrating just beneath the surface.

"What are you doing here, Chance?" I mentally cringe at the shaky sound of my voice.

He levels an intense gaze on me, his jaw hardening as he

slowly advances. "What's the matter, baby? You not happy to see me?"

I raise my chin in defiance even as I retreat, moving backwards to keep the space between us that's essential to my immediate survival. "I haven't heard from you in weeks. Why now—like this—in the middle of the night?"

The backs of my calves hit the coffee table and I start to fall, but Chance reaches out, his reflexes lightning-fast, and pulls me in by the lapels of my robe until our faces are mere inches apart. His drugging scent snakes around my head, and the heat from his body banishes the chill I've felt since the moment he left. I barely manage to swallow my sigh of relief as the warmth fills my veins.

"We have unfinished business, Jane. I'm here to tie up the loose ends."

I suddenly feel like a little worm wriggling on a big fucking hook. I wish I could say I didn't like it, that the notion made me scared or at the very least uncomfortable. But the flush creeping up my cheeks and the warmth pooling between my legs say otherwise.

"And what if I say I don't want my loose ends tied, huh? Then what?"

"I'd say I don't give a shit. And call you a liar."

My mouth drops open with a sound of protest, but that's as far as I get before he yanks the robe off my shoulders and shoves it roughly to the ground. Sparking with the electricity of a brewing storm, his eyes glare at my sleep clothes like he can burn them from my body with the sheer force of his will. "Take them off," he growls.

My head is spinning. I can't keep up with the maelstrom of thoughts whipping around in my brain: the ones ordering me to put a stop to this madness, the ones shouting at me to grab on, hook my legs around his waist and never let go. In the end, my stupid logic wins out. I wrap my arms across my middle and sidestep away from him. "No," I say, happily surprised my voice sounds stronger than I feel.

"Take them off or get fucked with them on."

Sweet baby Jesus. I almost give him my preference—*fucked with them on, please*—but come to my senses at the last second. "Just say whatever it is you're here to say, Chance. Then you can leave."

His head tilts slightly as though pondering my statement. "You expect me to talk? About what?"

"Stuff… Things…" I say helplessly, unable to articulate my thoughts when he starts to follow me, a stealthy predator stalking his prey. "You know," I try again, gesturing between us, "*this*."

Chance shakes his head and tsks like a disappointed parent. "That's where you're wrong, Jane. That's not how *this* works," he says, throwing my poor word choice back in my face. He crowds me against the wall, and I'm hit with a dose of déjà vu from that first night when I tried avoiding his advances. I'd been unsuccessful then, too. "That's not how we do things, you and I, is it?"

I know what he means. Asking him to clarify would only be a catalyst for the inevitable, an acceptance—no, an *invitation*—for what he plans to do. I know this as surely as I know my own name. Which is why I shock the logical part of myself when I set my jaw, meet his steely gaze, and demand, "And how exactly do 'we do things'?"

Pure wickedness. That's what flashes in his eyes and in the wry twist of his lips the split second before he pounces. His fingers plunge into my hair and fist against my scalp to yank my head back to his liking. I hardly have time to register the pleasure-pain that zings through the center of my body and pulses against my aching clit when he attacks my mouth, his tongue and teeth laying siege, plundering and claiming and branding me as his.

Desperate for him, I wind my arms around his neck and jump up at the same time he uses one hand to palm my ass and lift me. I lock my legs at the small of his back and pull him in as tight as I can. He uses the delicious weight of his body to pin me to the wall as he rocks his hips forward, pressing his stiff cock along the drenched seam of my thin boy shorts.

Reaching beneath me, he makes quick work of undoing the fly of his jeans, pulling the crotch of my boy shorts aside, and poising his erection at my entrance. I try to lower myself onto his thick shaft and feel him fill and stretch me as only he can, but he holds me in place with a strong arm banded around my waist, keeping my nirvana just out of reach.

"Please, Chance," I beg shamelessly. "Please please *please*."

"That's right, baby. *This* is how we fucking do things. You beg, and I do whatever the fuck I want." The husky sound of his deep voice next to my ear and his crude words threaten to unravel me, but I gather what little strength I have and trap my protests behind lips rolled between my teeth. Chance chuckles. "I see my little slut's stubborn streak has come out to play. I like that. Makes breaking you that much more satisfying."

I glare at him even as my arousal spikes to hear him call me his little slut again and at his promise to break me. It's exactly what I want. What I *crave*.

Without warning, he rams his hips upward, slamming his cock home so hard my vision blinks out for a few seconds. The myriad of sensations overwhelms me, wrenching a scream from my throat before he cuts it off with a hand over my mouth. The breaths I'm allowed to take through my nose ghost over his knuckles in swift puffs as the need to move on his cock becomes unbearable. Unable to take it any longer, I try to undulate my body against his, but the grips he has on my face and waist jolt me in warning.

"Don't you dare move," he growls. "Piss me off and I drop you to the floor. I'll make you watch as I fuck my fist until I come all over your pretty face. Then I'll tie your hands so you can't get yourself off. Is that what you want?"

I shake my head as vigorously as I can with him holding it hostage. It's not the first part of his threat I object to—I actually make a note to add that to my fantasy bucket list—but not getting to orgasm, not getting fucked by Chance now that I finally have him inside me again, would be the worst kind of torture.

"Good," he says, "because if there's one thing I enjoy the hell out of, it's fucking this tight pussy of yours. I want it to be mine. To have all the goddamn time—whenever and however I want it. You'd be my own personal fuck toy. Just you, Jane."

His words catapult me into mental ecstasy. Whimpering, I plead with my eyes to give us the physical euphoria we hunger for. But it doesn't matter how hard his baser instincts ride him; he won't surrender to them until he's good and ready.

"Yeah, I think you like that idea. But I wonder if you know what you're getting yourself into. You think I demanded a lot before, but you haven't seen anything yet. You'll be my only outlet for all the things lurking in my deviant fucking mind. My permanent little slut to do what I want with." He removes the hand over my mouth and asks, "You ready for that, Jane? Because I sure as fuck am."

Truthfully, he just described my idea of relationship heaven, but that stubborn streak he mentioned earlier makes me defiantly silent. He smacks my ass and I cry out in surprise, then relish the sweet pain. "*Answer me*. Is that what you want?"

When my body jerked in response to the spanking, I got a taste, a teasing reminder, of how phenomenal it feels to ride his cock. To feel his hard flesh pumping inside me again and again, the veins and ridges dragging over my sensitive walls and rubbing the spot that could send me flying apart in mere seconds.

It's more than enough to make me cave.

"*Yes*, goddamn it, that's what I want!"

"Good answer." With that, he makes good on his promise.

Over and over, Chance pistons his hips, fucking me for all he's worth. All I can do is hang on and accept his gloriously punishing thrusts. My inner thighs grow tender with bruises from the repeated jabs of his hipbones, and still I don't want him to stop. His hands are restless, alternating between pulling my hair, gripping my jaw, encircling my throat, and slapping my ass. If someone asked, I'd be hard-pressed to pick a favorite. Everything this man does to me turns me on to no end.

"That's it," he says. "Squeeze my cock as I fuck that hot cunt, baby. Fuck, I missed this. Missed fucking my little slut." I cry out and a fresh wave of arousal crashes through me when he yanks my head to the side and whispers harshly. "The next time you cause me to go without this pussy, I'll invite my friends over and let them have a turn. A good pussy should never go to waste. Just because you won't let me enjoy it doesn't mean others shouldn't."

Jesus Christ. The humiliation game jumped several levels with that image. Picturing him watching his friends pass me around like some kind of fuck toy is scorching hot like I can't even explain. It's not a fantasy I'd want played out in reality, and I know Chance is dead against sharing me, so it's safe to indulge in the taboo thoughts and implied degradation.

He must see it in my eyes because he curses under his breath and revokes the threat as quickly as he'd issued it. "Fuck that. You're mine. *Only mine.*"

The heat swirling in my belly is now a churning pit of fiery lava on the brink of erupting. My legs begin to tremble, and I clamp them harder around his waist in a futile attempt to squeeze my thighs together to ease the throbbing ache. Beads of sweat break out on his forehead and strained lines bracket his eyes and mouth, proving I'm not the only one struggling to hold out. But whereas he has an iron will, I'm fighting a losing battle.

As my climax nears its peak, I whimper and plead for the release only he can give me. His pace quickens, and he changes the angle so his pubic bone strikes my clit with every thrust. I moan and squeeze my eyes shut as the tingling races beneath my skin.

"Tell me you're mine!"

"*I'm yours!*" I scream, meaning it down to the marrow of my bones.

With a final roar ripped from his chest, he pushes home one last time, and we come together in the most intense orgasm of my life. After a minute and still clinging to each other, he moves lazily inside me, coaxing me through the aftershocks and drawing out our pleasure for as long as possible. Eventually, he eases me down his body and makes sure I'm steady on my feet. He readjusts my boy shorts then tucks himself back into his jeans, only bothering to pull up the zipper.

Tears prick the backs of my eyes, and I don't even know why. I suspect it's partially from the intensity of what we just shared after our time apart and partially from the uncertainty of where we go from here that's sitting like a brick in my stomach. Despite all that, I give him a watery smile. *Don't mind me. I'm just acting like a silly girl. Everything is totally fine.*

Sighing, he frames my face with the rough hands I love so much and stares deep into my eyes. "I fucked up the best thing in my life when I walked out that night. But I swear to you, I won't make that mistake twice. I'm sorry I hurt you, sweetness. So goddamn sorry."

I grab onto his wrists as though it will anchor me in this moment and give them a small squeeze. "I'm sorry, too. I never meant for you to think that your stripping is a deal breaker. As long as you're coming home to me, I don't care who you dance for."

A flicker of surprise skates over his features, then he smiles and places a kiss on each of my palms before holding them against his chest. "You're something else, you know that?"

I shrug and hope the twinge in my gut at the thought of him still working bachelorette parties doesn't show on my face. I said I didn't care. I didn't say I wouldn't like it. It's not something he'll do forever—I know that—so I'm happy to wait it out if it means we're together.

"You're a much better person than me," he continues, "because if I ever saw another man touch you like you saw your cousin touching me, I'd kill him."

"Believe me, the thought crossed my mind, but explaining it to my aunt would've been a pain in the ass."

The vibrations from his chuckle roll through me, warming me from the inside like fine brandy. "I like that you want me all to yourself, baby, and as it turns out, I have a weakness for giving you what you want. So, I'm done."

"Done?"

He nods. "You're the only woman I'm going to dance for ever again."

My heart leaps into my throat, and I struggle to swallow it back down so I can speak. "You're serious?"

"Dead serious. When I told you I didn't have a reason to stop, it was bullshit. *You* are my reason. But I'm not doing it just for you. I'm doing it for myself. I'm doing it for us." *He's choosing me. He's choosing us.* Chance softly brushes away my runaway tears with the backs of his knuckles. "I need to be with you, Jane. *I love you.*"

I freeze, my breath stuck in my chest. I know what this admission is costing him. Big, strong, unaffected Chance Danvers has flayed himself open and made himself vulnerable to a woman who hasn't yet given him any indication of whether she feels the same way. "You...love me?"

"More than I ever thought possible." He lowers his forehead to mine and watches the path his thumb makes over my lower lip. "Say something, sweetness," he says in a raspy voice. "Please."

"Say it again."

Hot tears fall past my lashes to stream down my face. Chance catches them with his thumbs and wipes them away. "I fucking love you."

Joy bursts from me in the form of a clipped laugh. "Of all the toe-curling, heart-stopping things you've ever uttered to me, *that* is my absolute favorite."

"Good, because from now on, I'm focusing my attention on two things: running my companies and loving the hell out of you." One side of his mouth lifts up—an attempt at his trademark cocky grin, but I can't help notice it's missing its usual confidence. "If you'll still have me."

Ah, and there it is. He's still unsure about everything, and I know it's because it all happened in the heat of the moment. The things he said to me were part of an act, part of the way we play together "in the bedroom," and now he's worried that maybe my words weren't genuine or that I feel differently now that lust is no longer clouding my judgment.

Gazing into the fathomless pools of midnight blue, I will him to hear the truth of what I'm about to say. "That first night you showed up, you not only fixed my sink, you fixed *me*. You offered to make my fantasies a reality, encouraged me to embrace my most secret desires. You taught me to be *shameless* and made me feel like I wasn't broken simply for wanting what I wanted. My heart will only ever beat for you,

Chance." I smile, the tears now streaming uncontrollably down my face. "I love you."

At last the shadows of doubt are chased away and his brilliant smile matches mine. Chance catches me up against him, lifting me off the floor, and kisses me long and hard until our need for air forces us to break apart.

"God, I fucking missed you," he rasps.

"Me, too. I missed *us*."

"Then let's not waste any more time getting *us* back."

He slowly lowers me until I'm once again on my feet, then takes a step back, reaches a hand behind his head, and pulls his shirt off in one smooth motion. My mouth waters with the desire to lick over his chest, the small buds of his nipples, and every ridge of muscle gracing his torso... But then I get distracted when his hands move to the fly of his jeans. My hungry gaze watches his fingers draw the zipper down, revealing what I didn't get to see when he took me like a madman before. I lick my lips in anticipation as he takes out his already hardening cock and starts stroking, making himself ready for me.

He pointedly looks at my clothes and jerks his chin. "Do what you should've done earlier and take them off, Jane. Show me what's mine."

My chest squeezes remembering he said something similar to me the first night I met him. *"...Get naked so I can see what's mine."* I'd wondered back then what it would be like to be claimed by him, and now I know. It's a feeling I can't begin to articulate and one I don't intend on taking for granted.

Eager to obey him, I shed my clothes quickly and wait for the next command. He whispers, "Breathtaking," and for the first time, I believe him. I push my shoulders back a bit more and stand a little taller—the result of my newfound confidence thanks to Chance. He can have any woman he wants, and he chose *me*.

My nipples pucker under the weight of his stare and a rush of warmth floods my sex, but the part of me that's swelling the most is my heart. This is where I belong, with this man, loving him and being loved *by* him. Whether he's stroking my hair as we fall asleep or he's pulling on it as he pounds me into the mattress, I know the love we have for each other is real, and it's forever.

"I hope you're ready to be sore as hell, baby," he says, his voice gravelly and the cords of his neck standing out with restraint, "because I plan on making up for the last several weeks of pent-up sexual frustration you caused me."

"Don't hold back on my account. You know I can take whatever you dish out."

Chance lets out a satisfied grunt that underscores his body's approval as a bead of pre-cum leaks from the dusky head of his dick. "I'm in a generous mood, so I'll give you a choice. We can get straight to the part where I bang your fucking brains out again, or you can wrap those lips around me and show me how much you missed my cock. What's it gonna be, Jane?"

"That's easy," I answer confidently, then smile as I sink to my knees.

He returns my smile with a feral one of his own, wraps a hand in my hair, then growls his signature response and my *second* favorite thing to hear him say to me. "Good answer."

Epilogue

CHANCE

I'm in the living room, flipping through a thousand channels and not finding a damn thing to watch. There are plenty of recorded shows on the DVR, but I won't watch any of them without Jane, and she's not home. She's having a GNO with Addison for the first time in forever, so it's just me and Romeo chilling together.

He keeps kneading the couch next to me, which has become Jane's spot since she moved in a few months ago, and giving me his whining meow, like if he acts pathetic enough I can magically make her appear. I pick him up and set him in my lap, scratching him behind the ears in a feeble attempt at consolation.

"I know, buddy, I miss her, too. But we're gonna have to pretend like she doesn't have our balls tucked under her pillow and suck it up for the next few hours, all right?" He answers in the same whine, and I'm about to lecture him when I hear the front door open and shut. Romeo bolts off my lap and rushes to the front hall. I mutter "traitor" and turn the TV off so I can focus on my girl, who walks into the room carrying said defector a second later.

"Hey, baby," I say, folding her into my arms as she sits in her spot next to me. I kiss her slow and deep like I do every time we've been apart for the day, then pull back and tuck her head against my shoulder. "Girls Night Out a bust?"

She sighs and nods under my cheek. "Yeah, Addie ended up having to work late. Again. That guy she works for is such a misogynistic asshole. I keep telling her there are other firms out there who would be happy to have her and who wouldn't treat her like such shit, but she feels obligated to stick with them because they gave her the internship when she was still getting her degree."

"Didn't she used to give you shit for working all the time and not taking breaks for fun?"

"Yeah, ironic, right? That's why she sent you over, though, so I can't be all that upset at her tactics," she says with a laugh.

"Maybe you should repay the kindness."

Jane pulls back to look at me, her brow furrowed, making that adorable crinkle above the bridge of her glasses. "What do you mean?"

A wicked grin hitches up the corner of my mouth as a plan starts to formulate. "I mean, what if we send over someone to help shake her loose, like she did you."

One of her eyebrows arches toward her hairline. "If you're talking about coming out of handyman retirement, Chance Danvers, so help me God I'm going to smack you."

I chuckle, loving the glimpse at the jealous streak that reminds me of why I gave up the stripper life and never looked back. The only woman I ever want to take my clothes off for is my Jane. "No, I was thinking more along the lines of another lawyer. One who could schedule a meeting in a conference room one of these nights when she's working late all by herself. One who might start loosening the constraints of his suit during the meeting to get comfortable and then might end up with it off all together."

Her beautiful brown eyes grow wide with excitement. "Oh my God," she says. "Roman."

"Not Roman," I answer with a wink. "Ruthless."

She claps her hands and nods. "Yes! Holy shit, that's pure genius." She grabs my face and plants a smacking kiss on my mouth. "One way or another, you always find a way to fix things. The handyman strikes again."

I shrug and grin as I pull out my phone and scroll for my friend's name. "I guess it's just in my nature." A couple of seconds later, with my girlfriend bouncing excitedly in my lap, Roman picks up. "Hey, Reeves. How'd you like to do me a favor?"

Acknowledgments

First and foremost, I need to thank my editor Liz Pelletier and my agent Nicole Resciniti. Both of them stuck by me with endless support when I was dealing with things that made writing almost impossible. Then they worked together to bring me back to life and hauled my ass out of career purgatory. I'm lucky to have them in my corner, and as great friends.

As always, to my husband and kids for dealing with way too many "Not now, I'm working" responses. Without their constant understanding, I wouldn't be able to do what I love.

To my sprinting partners who kick my ass on a regular basis: Rebecca Yarros, Cindi Madsen, MK Meredith, and Laura Wright. You girls rock my world. And my word counts.

To KP for being my best friend and being there when I need her. Every. Damn. Time.

And to the members of the Maxwell Mob, the greatest street team a girl could ask for. You keep me going. Love you all lots.

About the Author

New York Times and USA TODAY bestselling author, Gina L. Maxwell, is a shameless romance addict with no intentions of ever kicking the habit.

Growing up, she dreamed of helping people escape reality with her sublime acting abilities. It wasn't until college when she realized she had none to speak of, thereby derailing her lifelong plans. Another ten years would pass before she discovered a different means of accomplishing the same dream: writing stories of love and passion for romance addicts just like her.

Thanks to the support of her amazing family, Gina is now the Boss of the world's first organized romance mafia, the Maxwell Mob, and living her dream of bringing a little romantic fantasy to the world—one steamy novel at a time.

Visit and chat with Gina on all her social media homes:

www.ginalmaxwell.com

CPSIA information can be obtained
at www.ICGtesting.com
Printed in the USA
BVHW041028030822
643617BV00025B/123